Praise for *No Dawn for Men*:

"A rousing success, a thrilling adventure that does its clever frame story justice."
– Booklist

"Action-packed from the onset and never slowing down, fans of the two great authors and readers who appreciate a unique superbly written 1930s thriller will enjoy this unique, tense war drama."
– Midwest Book Review

"I blasted through this book."
– Cheryl's Book Nook

"*No Dawn for Men* again proves James LePore to be a superb crafter of thriller novels…. Highly, highly recommended!"
– Crystal Book Reviews

"Simply UN-PUT-DOWN-ABLE….Sinister, mystical, comical, and daring, *No Dawn For Men* will have you on the edge of your seat from start to finish. A gripping and captivating read that I highly recommended to all book lovers!"
– Reading for Pleasure

"If you are a fan of Tolkien or Fleming, then I highly suggest you pick up a copy of *No Dawn for Men*."
– Books: The Cheapest Vacation You Can Buy

An International Thriller Writers Thriller Award nominee

THE BONE KEEPERS

THE BONE KEEPERS

James LePore
and Carlos Davis

THE
ST●RY
PLANT

The Story Plant
Studio Digital CT, LLC
PO Box 4331
Stamford, CT 06907

Copyright © 2016 by James LePore and Carlos Davis

Jacket design by Barbara Aronica Buck
Cover painting © 2016 by Karen Chandler

Story Plant Paperback ISBN-13: 978-1-61188-222-3
Fiction Studio Books E-book ISBN-13: 978-1-943486-83-0

Visit our website at www.thestoryplant.com
Visit the author's website at www.jamesleporefiction.com

First Story Plant Paperback Printing: April 2016
Printed in the United States of America

0 9 8 7 6 5 4 3 2 1

Acknowledgments

I thank Carlos Davis for his great imagination, and Lou Aronica, for his encouragement and professional advice and eye throughout the writing of this series.

– J.L.

My thanks to Lou Aronica and Jim Lepore, Renaissance Men.

And to Tony Fingleton, Geri Rosenberger and Steve Loeshelle, Jamie Davis and Laura Armento who I hope will accept a collective expression of gratitude here.

And a special thanks to Charlie Gerli for his keen insight into things historical and otherwise.

– C.D.

<u>Dedication</u>

I dedicate this book to the memory of my grandparents, Vicenzo and Sadie LePore, Pasquale and Lena D'alessio. The journey began with them.

    – J.L.

For David Taylor
An incomparable friend

    – C.D.

<u>Prologue</u>
On The Adriatic Sea, May, 1930

Claudia, hoping to see land, lifted a corner of the tarp that covered the lifeboat, and peered out at the fog-shrouded sea that she would later learn was called the Adriatic. A strikingly handsome, dark-haired, dark-eyed sailor in the port city of Bari had smuggled her on board in exchange for her virginity, a bargain neither of them knew they were making at the time. Shocked at the amount of blood on the deck under the lifeboat, the sailor had pleaded with her to leave, but she had refused. Wherever the ship was going, she was going, as long as it was not Italy. The sailor, a boy himself, no more than eighteen or nineteen, his sun-bronzed, beautifully chiseled face suddenly ashen, his dark eyes glazed now not by lust but by fear, mopped up the blood with his shirt and slid out from under the lifeboat.

A half hour later, they were underway.

Claudia let the tarp down and rested her head on her canvas kit bag, recalling the look on his face when the young sailor saw the blood. "I thought you were a whore," he had said. "How old are you?"

"I *am* a whore," she said, "*now*."

She blamed the nuns at the orphanage for her new status, not the sailor. They had insinuated that her burgeoning body, rounding prematurely into womanhood at age twelve, was a sinful thing, a playground for the devil. She had honestly not known with any clarity what they meant, until her escape and her trek across the heart of the Italian peninsula, where several men had helped her while looking at her with an odd, intense look in their eyes. By the time she met the sailor in Bari, she knew what that look meant, or thought she did, and it was easy to get him to do what she wanted, which was to get on his ship, an Italian freighter that he told her stopped at many of the beautiful Greek islands.

Recalling the hurried moments after the sailor's last loud grunt and quick dismount, Claudia took her kit bag from behind her head, untied it, and removed the handkerchief she had used to wipe herself between her legs. The sailor, his face less ashen but still very grim, had come back an hour later, handed her a canteen, and said, "Our first stop is Corfu. I will sneak you off." She had drunk greedily and poured some of the water on her face, and then rested her head. She now uncapped and upended the canteen and poured the last of its contents onto the handkerchief. Turning onto her side, she did her best to scrub the blood from it. When the water was gone and she had scrubbed as much as she could, she looked at the square piece of simple cotton. Embroidered with an overlapping CR in the center, and pink roses in all four corners, it had been given to her the Christmas before last by one of the anonymous benefactors whose donations helped sustain the orphanage. Her only non-practical possession, she laid it on her chest to dry.

Along with her ignorance of male lust, she had also been ignorant, until now, of the workings of the female body. She had thought that being a virgin meant being pure of spirit. Now she knew otherwise. How could she have not known this? She would never be so foolish again. Her eyes dry, her mind clear, she fell asleep.

Some time later—she did not know how long—the blast of the ship's horn woke her, shocking her so much that she reflexively leapt upward, only to smash her forehead on the underside of the lifeboat. Another blast pinned her in fear to the deck. The third loud noise was not a horn, but the unmistakable boom of steel crashing against steel, followed by a severe pitching of the ship to its right side. This crash and pitch tore the lifeboat from the deck and tossed it, and Claudia, overboard like children's toys. Submerged in the cold sea, the first thing Claudia was aware of was a serpent gripping her waist. Keeping her mouth tightly shut, she opened her eyes and saw that the line securing the lifeboat to cleats on the deck had broken off and tangled itself around her body. The cleat was dangling some ten or fifteen feet below her, dragging her down. The heaving surface of the Adriatic was only a few feet above. *Not now*, she said to herself, as, her chest painfully close to bursting, she unraveled the rough hemp rope from her waist and swam to the surface, vomiting sea water when she got there, gulping in oxygen between heaves.

Looking around, she saw the freighter some fifty meters away through a break in the fog, listing so far on its side that its deck was taking on water. Was that land she saw just beyond the sinking ship? Before she could look again to be sure, she heard someone cry out behind her. Turning, she saw a young man with a bright red gash on his forehead about thirty meters away, swimming toward her with one arm, like a crippled crab. There was a white object of some kind a few meters in front of him that he seemed to be trying to reach. But with the use of only one arm he was losing ground on the object, which looked like a piece of painted wood bobbing on the sea. Was it her sailor? *That black hair, those black eyes.* Had he come back to save her when the crash occurred? Still heaving the Adriatic out of her lungs, struggling to keep her head above water—she had never even seen the sea let alone learned how to swim—she looked around frantically for something to cling to, something she could use to propel herself toward the sailor. The lifeboat had to be close by. But it wasn't. The ship was now gone behind a wall of fog. Frightened by the sudden silence, she swiveled to look for the one-armed swimming man. At first she saw nothing but thick mist and swelling sea. Then something rose into view on one of the swells. A log? A man floating head down? Then the thing she saw, whatever it was, slipped into a trough and was lost in the fog.

Her arms suddenly very weak, Claudia arched her back to try to stay afloat. She rose and fell on the swells this way, suspended in time and space, gulping in spray in the troughs and spitting it out on the swells, getting weaker with each passing moment. "Now, Lord," she said, "take me now." And then something bumped into her from behind. Turning, she saw it was a life ring, a piece of cork covered in white canvas. With the last of her strength, she slipped it over her head and under her arms. Sobbing, her heart beating so hard she could feel it against her chest, she clung like death to the life ring. Stroking it, she noticed the stenciled lettering on its curved surface: *Queen of Heaven.*

As a child, Mary had been the saint Claudia felt closest to, the Queen of Heaven, the Mother of Sorrows, who she could talk to during the many lonely days and nights of her captivity. She did not know what irony was until this moment. She had been saved by Mary, the queen of all saints, the all-compassionate mother of heaven and earth, who could have been a lifelong friend, but who, now that Claudia Roselli was a whore, she could never talk to again.

Gathering her strength, she kicked in the direction of the spit of land that had once again come into view. *You had another savior, Claudia,* she said to herself, certain that the handsome sailor who had made her into a whore and the one who had sent her the life ring were one and the same. Her sailor had introduced himself as Figaro. "*Al vostro servizio*," he had said when they met, smiling broadly, his dark eyes dancing. She knew this wasn't his real name, that he was making a joke of some kind. Perhaps having to do with the famous opera that every Italian knew of, even twelve-year-old girls in orphanages? She did not know for sure, nor did she know what a play on words was, nor how ironically significant this one was.

"Thank you, Figaro," she said out loud now, kicking even harder, *or whatever your name is. May you rest in peace.*

PART I

THE PROSTITUTE

1.

Northern Judea, July 15, AD 13

The arid foothills outside the small city of Scythopolis were like a second home to the boy. He hunted partridge and quail with a slingshot, herded his father's goats here, and used a series of hidden caves to do what thirteen-year-old boys do: escape to daydream of an adventurous and romantic future. Adventurous because his father hated the occupying Romans. With a group of his landowning peers, Jacob Beit She'an met often to drink wine and talk about casting off the yoke of Rome. Sometimes, with too much wine in their bellies, there was talk of armed rebellion. Until, that is, someone less drunk than the others pointed out that their weapons consisted of slingshots and poor quality hunting bows. No match for a wall of Roman infantrymen with their tooled armor, interlocking shields, and deadly *gladii*, honed to a razor's edge, always at the ready.

Perhaps, the boy would often allow himself to think, while lying quietly in a cool cave, the harsh desert far away, *I will someday find a way to arm our people, to destroy the Romans, to make my father proud.*

Today the boy was helping his father mark their property with iron stakes. He knew where most of the old stone markers were and, after scraping off the dirt and grime with one of the ubiquitous rough rocks that covered the desert floor, so that they could confirm the family insignia, he and Jacob took turns pounding the stakes into the hard, often stubbornly impenetrable ground. As they worked in the hot sun, they saw dust rising on a nearby plain, and could occasionally hear men barking out short sentences.

At noon they found a small patch of shade, where they sat and silently ate their midday meal of figs, goat cheese and bread.

"Dogs," said Jacob, spitting on the ground, after they had finished eating.

This pronouncement surprised the boy, not by its guttural vehemence—he knew how his father felt about the Romans, who they both knew were the ones raising the dust and shouting in the distance—but that it been spoken at all. Jacob Beit She'an was not a talkative man. He and his son had often spent full days like this working in the desert with only one or two words passing between them, and those utilitarian. Once, the boy had taken ill while they were searching for one of their goats, a kid whose mother had died. Seven at the time, he had been afraid to say anything. His white-haired father was as remote and fearsome to him as Mount Hermon, the snow-covered old gray man, which they could see in the far distance on clear days. Finally he had collapsed. Jacob had taken his son's head in his hands and looked intently into his eyes. "Simon," he said. The boy could not speak. The hot sun had taken away his voice. And then Jacob had lifted him swiftly into his arms and carried him home, a two-mile trek over rocky terrain under the same blazing sun that had rendered the boy senseless.

"They use my land to train," said Jacob. "They dig for wells where there is no water. They kill my goats for sport. And then they charge me for doing this."

Simon was stunned. This was the longest statement his father had ever made directly to him.

"We need a king to match their emperor," Jacob went on. "A messiah."

"Father . . ."

"Don't speak, son. I am just an old man, and powerless. My words will not free us. There will be no messiah."

"I . . ."

"Hush," said Jacob. "They are closer."

The sounds drifting from the Roman camp were indeed closer, the grunts of the troops and the orders of the centurions leading the training much more intelligible.

"We need water," said Jacob. On the ground at their feet were two goatskin water bags, one full, the other half full. Simon glanced at them and then back to his father.

"The sun is without mercy today," Jacob said. "We will need more."

"Yes, Father."

"The spring you told me about. Is it near?"

"Just over that hill."

"Go," said Jacob, "take the half-empty bag."

2.
Rome, July 13, 1943, 5 p.m.

"His Holiness," said Cardinal Federico Falco, "tells me that you heard his confession when he was in England in 1901."

"Yes."

"And again when he visited in 1913."

"Yes."

"Extraordinary."

Father Francis Xavier Morgan nodded.

"Your work here has been invaluable," said the cardinal.

"God has blessed me."

"This subterranean chamber, how did you locate it?"

"I was looking for missing records."

"What kind of records?"

"Papal letters."

"What years?"

"1734, 1735."

"Why?"

"They were missing from the Manuscripts and Archives Library. I was told to collate and organize."

"They were in the chamber?"

"Yes."

"Who told you about it?"

"Sister Rafaela."

"Who is she?"

"She helps Father Alfonso, the librarian."

"I've never heard of her."

"She's older than even I am. In her nineties."

"How did she know about this secret room?"

Father Morgan hesitated. He had heard rumors of Falco's reputation for intimidation, and physically he certainly was intimidating. Aged fifty or so, he was austerely dark and handsome, with no trace of humor or sentimentality in his piercing eyes. At first he had been pleasant enough, speaking softly, even respectfully, but now there was something about Cardinal Falco's tone of voice that did not seem quite right. Father Morgan thought highly of Sister Rafaela, who had been his only friend in Rome these past months. It bothered him to think that Falco might descend upon her.

"Rest easy, Father," said the cardinal. "Permit me to ask you this: Did Father Alfonso know you were entering this chamber?"

"I don't know."

"Have you told him?"

"No."

"And Sister had the keys?"

"Yes."

"She probably knows more about our archives than Father Alfonso," said Falco.

"She has devoted her life to them," Father Morgan replied, still unsure where this was going. Cardinal Falco was smiling, but not very convincingly.

"Thank you for bringing the letters to me," the cardinal said.

"I thought of course I should."

"Did you make copies?"

"No."

"Did you show them to Sister Rafaela?"

"No."

"Does she know you took them?"

"No, I . . ."

"Yes?"

"No, nothing."

"You seem worried, Father. Please, desist. I know of this so-called secret chamber. It used to be a holding room for papers to be vetted and discarded. You must have seen other odd documents."

"Yes, I did."

"Anything referring to the subject matter of these letters?"

"No."

"Have you spoken of these letters to anyone?"

"No."

"You must not. You can understand the harm it would cause to spread such a rumor."

"Of course."

"Bishop Benedetti was excommunicated and committed suicide in 1736."

"I did not . . ."

"He was stealing from the papal accounts, and then he tried to extort money, large sums, from the Holy See. These letters were part of his scheme."

"Goodness."

"I will have the room cleaned out. It is long overdue."

On the massive mahogany table in the center of the prelate's office were a series of beautifully scrivened letters between Pope Clement XII and his papal nuncio in Constantinople, one Archbishop Patricio Benedetti. Both men glanced at them.

"Clement also issued a decree," Falco continued, "excommunicating anyone who spread the lies contained in Benedetti's correspondence."

"I see."

"Yes. Of course you do," said the cardinal.

The two men eyed each other, the letters spread out on the table between them.

"That will be all, Father," said Falco. "Please continue your work."

ooooo ooooo ooooo

The cardinal, his thin lips grim, his hawk-like eyes hooded, watched the English priest leave and quietly close the door behind him, then picked up his phone and dialed three numbers.

"Carlo," he said when his call was answered.

"Yes?"

"How long has Alfonso Vitale been with us?"

"The librarian?"

"Yes."

"Ten years."

"How did he get his job?"

"He was appointed by Pius XI."

"You don't say? The great librarian himself. May he rest in peace. So, Father Alfonso is no longer protected in high places."

"Yes. *And . . .?*"

"It's time for him to go."

"Go?"

"Yes, re-assigned."

"When?"

"Immediately."

"What shall I tell him?"

"Tell him we know about the whores he sneaks in after hours."

"What did he do?"

"He let a ninety-year-old nun have the run of the Vatican archives."

"Re-assigned where?"

"Send him to a university library; any place nearby will do."

"He'll complain. His life here has been very good. He thinks he has friends."

"His life here has been *too* good. I will sign the papers. He won't complain when he sees my seal."

"It will be done."

3.
Galilee, March 26, AD 33, 11 a.m.

It is bigger today, and calmer, Simon said to himself as he walked along the rocky scree at the northern edge of the Sea of Galilee. Yesterday's storm had whipped the sea's surface to a froth and driven the fishermen that plied it daily into its shores; and the torrents that had fallen from the sky had seemed to fill it to its brim, enlarging it by at least half. Simon, born in Scythopolis to the north, had spent the last week in this part of Galilee, exploring the hill country that climbed up from the sea toward the Syrian Heights, looking for likely places to locate burial caves for his new client, the enigmatic, and rich, Joseph of Arimathea. Old Joseph's house, where he had stayed the nights and been treated well, was spacious and comfortable, but startlingly simple. A clever ruse, Simon thought, to fool his neighbors in their gaudy villas, most of them jealous and greedy Romans. Or was it true piety? The kind that so enraged Joseph's other neighbors, the Sadducees, themselves wealthy and greedy and suspicious of any fellow aristocrat whose religious fervor was not quite as superficial as theirs?

Turning from the shoreline, Simon began to crisscross his way up a stony outcrop, thinking to get a better view of the country around the small, heart-shaped Sea of Galilee. Rich Romans had settled in this area as well, and he wanted to see

29

if he could spy the villa belonging to the man he was to meet with later today, to discuss the purchase of a tract of barren, seemingly useless land for Joseph. At the top of a large, flat boulder he turned and saw, some fifty meters away, a group of people gathered around a man standing and speaking to them on the top of a small, gently sloping hill. The man was perhaps the same age as Simon, thirty-three, and a bit taller, but with the same dark skin and beard and piercing eyes as the majority of the native men in the sun-baked, arid portion of the world that the Romans called Judea, a name the local people pronounced Yahuda.

Stepping softly, Simon started across the small flat-land between the two rocky hills. Halfway there he stopped or, rather, *was* stopped. By what? Looking up, he realized it was the silence surrounding the listeners, the utter silence in which, and through which, the man's voice permeated like the voice of heaven itself, like one of the gods the Greeks had gone on so much about and that Simon had derided all his life. Simon spoke Greek, and thought he had forgotten the Aramaic of his childhood. But when he joined the crowd he understood everything the man was saying in that ancient language. But what was the meaning of these strange declarations? *Surrender, unworthiness, humility, suffering* . . . How could these things make us happy? How could these things be the blessings this man spoke of with such simple conviction?

4.
Rome, July 16, 1943, 11 p.m.

Claudia Roselli had designed her own coat of arms: her initials stylishly interlocked—the C on the left slightly above and overlapping the R on the right—with a pink rose in the space where the lower curve of the C intersected the top corner of the R. Some men had of course seen the striking resemblance. Young Luca Segreto, a new client from a wealthy, Jewish family, had not, but then how many vaginas had he seen? Really seen? Her older clients, yes. Many of them had made a close study of the pink rose, with its sweet nectar, that had afforded them so much pleasure. The younger ones though, like Luca—who, at the moment, was sleeping soundly, drooling on the *CR* crest embroidered on her pillow—could not control their hot blood. They plunged without looking, often exploding on contact. One day he would look closer, become a connoisseur perhaps. Not now though. Now he was just a typical nineteen-year-old male, with the unearned saving grace this demographic enjoyed: he could climax three or four times a night without much in the way of a breather in between. Older men Claudia charged by the hour, younger by the orgasm. Sitting up in bed, gazing at the Jewish Adonis sleeping next to her, Claudia stroked his long, dark hair, splayed carelessly on her satin pillow, wiped away his drool and pondered the opportunity he offered.

Over wine, and in between lovemaking, with the stricken look in his beautiful, dark-brown eyes that Claudia had seen many times in many other young men's eyes, Luca had revealed much more of himself than was necessary in order to complete their basically simple transaction of sex for money. She had mixed a drop of laudanum with his last glass of wine, something she did with many of her clients who were spending the night, as the better they slept the better she slept. With a look of adoration in her eyes, Claudia had listened as Luca told her that he was the only son of a very rich banker, living on an estate on the Appian Way in the lush, rolling hills just south of Rome, that his father was ill and likely to die very soon. These facts alone made him extremely interesting, but something he said just before passing out, his tongue completely loosened by the opium, had startled her. She usually discouraged the falling-in-love business. It made things too complicated. She would much rather lust brought her clients back, not love. Now, thinking of how slowly her savings had accrued, of the news of the Americans and British sweeping through Sicily and now landing in Italy, Claudia saw clearly that she would not get many more opportunities like the one presented by Luca Segreto. She decided she would encourage her new client's budding love for her, a simple task for a woman of twenty-five with an angelic face, a body made for pleasure and vast experience of men of all ages and walks of life.

Claudia knew her young men. The tincture of laudanum would wear off in a few hours. Luca would awake and they would make love again, perhaps more than once, before the new day truly dawned. When he left, she would consider what to do with the stupefying "secret" he had revealed to her. It couldn't possibly be true. But, then again, there had been something in the boy's eyes—and voice—that gave her great pause. He was terrified. *In vino—and laudanum—veritas*, she thought.

One of Claudia's regular clients was a pharmacist who paid her fees in kind with tiny vials of pure-grade laudanum, which she used tactically with certain clients, and which she occasionally indulged in herself. She had had trouble sleeping since, at the age of twelve, she had been woken with a crash while dozing under a lifeboat and dumped head-first into the Adriatic Sea. Tonight, thoughts of large sums of money swirling in her head, of escape from the life of a whore, she placed a drop of the liquid opium in her own wine. The tincture was so pure that, indeed, only a tiny drop was needed for her to become quickly drowsy.

Though images of money, *couture* clothes and beautiful surroundings danced in her head, her last thought before falling into the arms of Morpheus was a strange one: *God—if you still exist—help us.*

5.
Galilee, March 26, AD 33, 7 p.m.

"Your cave is nothing like the one at Machpelah," said Simon.

"So you know your Tanakh. I would have guessed otherwise," replied Joseph.

"Learned early, it is hard to unlearn."

"Why unlearn it?"

"They are tales to frighten children and yoke adults."

Old Joseph put down his wine goblet and looked across the small, open-air sitting room to the young man who had today purchased for him a cave on the outskirts of Jerusalem not far from the hill the natives called Golgotha, the Place of the Skull. "You have put a wall up against God," he replied.

Simon sat up a bit straighter in his cushioned bench, but did not answer.

"I am what you see," said Joseph, "but you are not."

"What am I then?"

"Something happened to you."

"Are you a prophet, a seer?"

"No. I am an old man who will die soon."

"Is the cave for you? It is a poor man's grave."

"No."

"Who, then?"

"Tell me first, what happened to you?"

Simon rose and went to the stone railing that overlooked Joseph's hillside vineyard. He gazed for a moment then, turning to face Joseph, said, "God has put a wall up against *me*."

"Perhaps he did it for a reason."

"When I was thirteen, the Romans killed my father as I watched. My mother and two sisters were taken as slaves."

Joseph kept his face expressionless.

"A common story," said Simon, a wry smile on his rugged, sunburned face.

Old Joseph chose to ignore this comment and the hints of both deep despair and deep cynicism in the younger man's voice. He too had sunk to those same depths, but something had happened recently to awaken him, something he could only describe as a miracle.

"Why?" Joseph asked. "What was your father's crime?"

"He was thought to be involved in a local rebellion."

"Was he?"

"No, but he would not pay tribute to Augustus. He said to anyone who would listen that the Romans would eventually impoverish Judea and destroy the temple."

"Was he a man of property?"

"Yes, like you, and, like you, pious. He kept the covenant."

"How do you know I am pious?" Joseph asked.

"There are not many of you."

Old Joseph smiled. "There are traps everywhere," he said.

"You are not proud, Joseph of Arimathea."

"The Lord forgive me if I am," Joseph replied. "What happened?" he asked.

"We were in the desert, marking property. I was in a small canyon getting water. As I was climbing out, I heard rough voices. I crouched and saw my father on his knees, surrounded by Roman soldiers. One was standing over him.

"He killed him. He cleaved him with his sword, from shoulder to heart."

"An honorable death."

"Honorable?"

"They could have taken his head, or dragged him away to be crucified. Have you seen a man crucified?"

"No."

"They scourge him first so that the flies will increase his suffering."

Simon, his sharp eyes darkening for a second, did not answer. *Remembering*, Joseph thought. "How did you live?" he asked.

"I slept in a cave that night. The next morning, I crept home. On the door a paper was nailed: *Taken As Slaves For Rebellion Against The Emperor.* I started walking south. One day I came upon two women who could not get into a burial site. A rockfall had covered the entrance. I helped them move the rocks. They gave me food and water. I was starving."

"Is that how you learned your trade?"

"Yes."

"Are you married?"

"I married the daughter of one of the women who saved me."

"Are there children?"

"No."

"Perhaps there will be."

"My wife . . ." said Simon.

"Yes?"

"She has had several stillbirths."

Joseph stepped quietly over to Simon and stood next to him. Below them in a small, flat valley were perhaps fifty meticulously aligned rows of grape vines, their clusters of tiny white flowers just beginning to bloom. They were surrounded on three sides by twisted but sturdy olive trees, standing guard against the biting, destructive winds that sometimes swept across this part of Judea.

"Some years my vintners work feverishly and yet the yield is pitiful," said Joseph. "Other years they do nothing and the grapes multiply to a thousandfold."

Simon remained silent as both men gazed down on the valley covered with the golden rays of the setting sun.

"You are afraid," said Joseph.

"Yes, I—"

"It is in God's hands," said Joseph, interrupting, "not yours."

"I—"

Simon was interrupted again, not by his gracious host, but this time by Joseph's household steward, a swarthy, clean-shaven man whom Joseph had purchased as a slave but treated like a brother.

"Shemayon Keppa," said the steward.

"Peter?"

"Yes, Master. He says it is urgent."

"Bring him in."

6.
Rome, July 17, 1943, 10 a.m.

"Bless me, Father, for I have sinned," said Claudia Roselli.

"We can dispense with the preliminaries," Cardinal Federico Falco replied. "Unless you are really here to confess."

Claudia remained silent. She had not been to confession, a real confession, that is, since she was confirmed at the age of twelve, some thirteen years ago. The next day she escaped from the orphanage where she had been raised since birth.

"No," she replied finally. "It would be pointless."

"Pointless?"

"I will only sin again very quickly. Perhaps during my penance I will have impure thoughts."

Cardinal Falco, hidden behind his partition, remained silent.

"Yes, Father, whores have impure thoughts."

"You mock the sacrament."

"So you say. Perhaps I honor it too much."

"Why are you here?"

"I have heard something."

"From a client?"

"Yes."

"What is it?"

Claudia told the cardinal what Luca Segreto had told her.

After a pause that struck Claudia as too long, the priest chuckled and said, "I have not heard that one before."

"Good," said Claudia. "It is nothing."

"Nothing."

Another pause.

"I will go then," said Claudia.

"Who was the client, may I ask?" said Falco.

"I can't reveal that."

"Why not? You have taken no vow."

"Of secrecy, you mean?"

"Yes."

"I haven't, but if I went about revealing my clients' identities I would soon have no clients."

"Exceptions can be made."

"Why? I thought you said it was nothing."

"You are correct," said the cardinal, without pausing this time. "I was just curious." She could not see him, but Claudia could feel him smiling, beaming even, as if he were reassuring a frightened child, no *l'uomo nero* here. *Nothing to worry about, my sweet.*

"You, of all people," said Claudia.

"You never fail to remind me."

"Priests are human."

"My dear, Claudia . . ."

"I understand."

"Understand what?"

"Better for your conscience to pay me for information than for sex."

The cardinal sat mute.

"Although," the voluptuous young prostitute said, "I obtain the information I sell you from sex." *Don't patronize me, Rico,* Claudia said to herself.

"I am sorry I hurt you," Falco said.

Now it was Claudia's turn to be mute. She had fallen in love with the darkly handsome and powerful Falco when, in 1940, at the age of twenty-two, she had returned to Rome, after ten years at a high-class bordello in Athens. No lover

40

had hurt her since. Indeed, she had had no other real lovers since Falco, then a bishop and the papal nuncio to Mussolini's government, had broken off their affair in 1941. Since then she had lived enough to learn one of life's immutable truths, that there is equal pain on both sides of a broken love affair.

"I apologize," she said, keeping her tone light. "You are as devout as any of my clerical clients. More, actually." *Do you still love him, Claudia?* she asked herself. *Is that why you have to torture him? Is that why you call him "Father," to pierce his heart? Is that why you mention other clerical clients, to inflame his jealousy?*

"Unlike you, I confess regularly," said Falco.

"Perhaps I will too, one day. But not now. Now I must go."

"Don't go yet."

"Of course not. What is it?"

"I must ask you a favor?"

"Please. It will be my pleasure."

"Have you told anyone else of this young man's secret?"

"No."

"Indulge me. Do not."

"But Father, I thought—"

"I lied. I have heard it before. It is a slander spread by the enemies of the Church, suppressed for many years. Now it rears its head. You know of course that Herr Hitler hates the Church."

"I thought we were allies?"

"Do not jest, Claudia."

Claudia had indeed been toying with the prelate. He had been forced to show his hand, which she knew he would not have done except for the gravest of reasons, and which she also instinctively knew placed her in harm's way. Playing the innocent, though she knew he would see through it, was the best she could do. Caught, she remained silent.

"You are correct," Falco said. "We are allies. But we won't be for long. When we turn against them, they will blame the

Holy Father. They will want to destroy him, and the Church. This so-called secret is nonsense, but if they hear of it, they will use it to their advantage. They are slaughtering and plundering all over Europe. The Church has no army. We are as naked and vulnerable as Christ on the cross."

Claudia, thinking, *Who is this Luca Segreto?*, absorbed this.

"*E così?*" said the cardinal.

"*Certo*, Monsignor."

ooooo ooooo ooooo

Not now, Rico Falco said to himself, as he exited the confessional in the deserted, dimly lit Archbasilica of St. John Lateran. *Dear Lord, not now of all times.* Falco, in the simple habit of a parish priest, nodded to his assistant, who was kneeling in a nearby pew. This man, Carlo Fiore, also a priest, burly and thickly muscled, his face ravaged by a youthful battle with smallpox, rose quickly.

"Where is she?" the cardinal asked. He had expected to see Claudia kneeling in a nearby pew, solemnly whispering her penitential prayers, following through, as he had instructed her at the beginning of their new relationship, with their confessional charade. "Assume you are being followed," he had told her. "Do your penance, genuflect at the altar, receive communion the next day."

"She went straight out," Fiore answered.

They made their way through a maze of back passages to a little-used rear entrance whose ancient stone portico was covered with a century's growth of vines. Standing in the dappled shadow of these vines, the cardinal gave his assistant a simple order: "Bring her to me."

7.
Rome, July 17, 1943, 10 p.m.

"Alfonso," said Claudia Roselli. "It's always a pleasure to see you."

"And you," said Alfonso Vitale, the former Vatican librarian. "Your home is lovely, as I suspected it would be."

"Thank you." *You don't have to flatter me*, Claudia thought. *As long as you pay, you'll get what you came for.*

"Do all of your visitors use your secret entrance?" Vitale asked.

"Yes," Claudia replied, "especially priests." This was not true. The entrance through the rear of the apartment building next door, reached via a labyrinth of forgotten Roman streets and alleys, she had reserved for the wealthiest of her clients, her *pezzi grossi*, those who wanted their clandestine life to be stay clandestine. She had only started using it herself this morning when she realized she had a stalker, a priest, whom she had spotted as she made her way home from her "confession" at St. John Lateran, and who she lost in the maze of streets leading to her secret entrance. "You have never come to me before," she said, changing the subject. "Are you on holiday?"

"I have been reassigned."

"Re-assigned?"

"Yes."

"What happened? Why?"

"I don't know exactly, but it was Falco, the Hawk himself, who ordered it."

"You have friends, surely, Alfonso." *Falco.*

"No one who would be willing to be clawed by the Hawk."

Father Alfonso had entered Claudia's small but elegant apartment, placed one hundred US dollars in twenties on an ornate marble credenza, taken off his collar and sat down in a velvet-covered easy chair in her parlor. The apartment was on the fifth floor of a building a few blocks from the Campo de' Fiori, which had evolved over the centuries from a large flower market to an outdoor housewares bazaar. From the window near his chair the priest could see, if he was interested, which he wasn't, a sliver of the piazza, where many of the merchants were re-opening their stands for the evening's trade.

"Where are you working?" Claudia asked

"I'm an assistant librarian at Sapienza University."

"You seem so downcast."

"I am."

Claudia, tall and thin, with a flaring rear end and large, perfectly shaped breasts, had been slowly undressing while they talked. She was naked now, her full beauty on display. The late afternoon sunlight streaming in from the nearby window cast her in a golden, other-worldly glow.

"I will cheer you up," she said, kneeling at Alfonso's feet. "But first I must ask for a favor."

"A favor?"

"Yes."

"In lieu of cash?" The priest, chunky, balding, his flesh pasty from so many years among the Vatican's immense collection of books and papers, was eyeing the bills on the credenza.

"*Tu sei pazzo*," said Claudia, half frowning and half smiling. "My clients always pay." She had leaned back as she spoke, as if hesitant to commit to the act that she knew Alfonso Vitale, indeed all men, loved so much.

"What kind of favor?" Alfonso said. "I will try to help you, of course." He was eyeing her the way any man would, ready, as most men would be, to promise anything.

"Do you still have the keys to the archives?" Claudia asked.

"The *Vatican* archives?"

"Yes, my dear Alfonso, the Vatican archives."

"Yes, I took a set away with me."

"I need some documents."

"You want me to steal papal documents?"

"Yes."

"My dear Claudia . . ."

Claudia leaned in and again gave him her half smile, half frown.

"What kind of documents?" the priest asked.

"Documents about Christ's remains."

"Christ's remains? Claudia, there *are* no remains."

"I agree, but these documents refer to them."

"Where are they?"

"Surely, Alfonso, you of all people must know where the Church keeps its secret papers."

The librarian did not reply. He had his hand on Claudia's head now, running his fingers through her long, silky, dark-brown hair.

"I will make it worth your while," Claudia said.

"How?"

"Are you angry at Falco?"

"Yes."

"These documents will destroy him."

Vitale stopped stroking Claudia's head and nodded.

"I can sell them for a lot of money," said Claudia. "Which I will share with you."

"How much money?"

"Enough for you to buy back your old job."

The priest's lips were pursed now. *Revenge and money,* Claudia thought, eyeing him, *and now sex.*

"Do you remember my friend Gina?" she said. "You were interested in her joining us?"

"Yes."

Claudia smiled and arched her eyebrows.

"*Will* she?"

"She'll do anything I ask. And I will pay her fee."

Claudia had placed her breasts on the priest's knees. Now she brushed them gently along the inside of his thighs.

"Claudia . . ."

"*Va bene*, Alfonso," said Claudia, reaching for the priest's belt buckle. "You drive a hard bargain. You will have *me* for free as well, anytime you wish."

8.

Galilee, March 26, AD 33, 7 p.m.

"Peter," said Joseph.

"Master."

"This is Simon of Scythopolis."

Simon and Peter looked at each other.

"We have met," said Peter.

"Yes," said Simon, "today, near the sea. There was a preacher. A man from Nazareth named Jesus."

"The tomb is for him," Joseph said to Simon. Then to Peter: "Simon purchased a burial site for me today near Golgotha."

The three men were standing near a fountain in a corner of the atrium-style, open-air room at the rear of Joseph's hillside house. The sound of trickling water punctuated the silence that followed this announcement by Joseph. In that silence Simon watched as Joseph and Peter exchanged glances. Was there consternation in the younger man's dark eyes? Surprise? Fear? Who was this Jesus of Nazareth, who spoke with such power, whose burial site was so bleakly situated, and who had as a benefactor a rich man like old Joseph?

"I will not live long," Joseph continued. "The Master will need a burial place."

"The Master?" said Simon.

"It may be needed sooner than you think," said Peter.

"What has happened?" Joseph asked.

Peter hesitated, looking from the old man to Simon.

"There will be no secrets," said Joseph. "Simon is my guest and has been sent here by God."

"What god do you speak of?" said Simon. "Do you mean the god of silver? If so, you are correct." Simon immediately regretted his lack of control, acknowledging to himself for the first time that Joseph had quickly become a substitute for his father, whose blind piety had made an orphan of his only son at the age of thirteen. It caught him short when he was forced to face the fact that his anger was as raw and painful now as it was twenty years ago when he arrived home to find that his mother and sisters were gone forever and that he was alone in the world.

"Joseph . . ." said Peter.

"Go on," old Joseph said to Peter, his voice deep and firm.

"He preached again this afternoon," said Peter. "There was a large gathering. He said that the scribes and the Pharisees sit in Moses' seat. We are to listen to their instructions and to follow them. But not to do as they *do*, for they do not practice what they teach. He said we should not call them rabbi, for there is only one teacher and we are all students."

"Not to call them rabbi," said Joseph. "Go on."

"He sent James to bring him an ass and a colt. He says his time is near."

"*Say to daughter Zion,*" said Joseph, his voice soft now, almost whispering, "*behold your king comes to you, meek and riding on an ass, and on a colt, the foal of a beast of burden.*"

"Zechariah," said Simon, reflexively.

Joseph and Peter turned to look at Simon. "My father—" said Simon, but Joseph interrupted him.

"How near?" he asked Peter.

"Who is this man?" Peter said, staring hard at Simon.

"He is a bone keeper," Joseph answered. "He has found a tomb for me today, and will stay to fulfill his commission."

"My father," said Simon, "was keen on the messianic prophecies. He beat me if I did not learn them."

"How near, Peter?" said Joseph, ignoring this statement from Simon.

"He says soon," Peter responded. "I believe he intends to enter Jerusalem in the coming days."

"What commission?" Simon asked.

"I will want the bones preserved as if they were the bones of a king," Joseph replied. "Indeed, they are the bones of a king."

"Whose bones?" Simon asked.

"The bones of Jesus the Nazarene," said Peter. "King of the Jews."

Simon shook his head almost imperceptibly. King of the Jews, indeed. And yet he had heard the man preach and was mesmerized, as was the entire throng, all standing and listening to a man whose voice seemed to make time stop, to swing open the door to eternity. He said nothing. He was anxious to fulfill old Joseph's commission and return home to his wife, who was with child once again, perhaps for the last time, one way or the other.

"Take this," said Joseph, breaking into Simon's thoughts.

"What is it?"

"A list of instructions for the burial."

Simon took the parchment from Joseph and scanned it.

"*The instruments of his death,*" he said. "I don't understand."

"He will be killed," said Joseph, "by the Romans or the council, perhaps both. Whatever they use, whatever pieces of it you can find, place in the ossuary. I have signed it and sealed it, as has Peter."

Simon again shook his head. The sooner he was away from here, the better.

"And you must sign this," said the old man. "It is an oath."

Simon again read what was handed to him. "And if I refuse?" he said.

"Take it with you," said Joseph. "There will be a time when you will be eager to sign it."

"I don't . . ."

"You don't understand, but you will," said Joseph, "when your son takes his first breath."

9.
Oxford, July 18, 1943, 10 a.m.

Tears in his eyes, Professor John Ronald Reuel Tolkien stood in full sunlight on a patch of grass at Holywell Cemetery and watched as the casket containing the body of Robert Quilter Gilson III, was lowered into the ground. Full to the brim, no one had been buried at Holywell for twenty years, but the War Office had interceded and leave was granted to inter young Robert next to his father, a friend of Professor Tolkien's youth who had been killed by a shell on the first day of the Battle of the Somme in July of 1916. Memories of Bob Gilson, suppressed these many years, flooding back, had loosed Tolkien's tears. There were others crying openly among the mourners at the gravesite. It would be hard not to cry for the local lad, a paratrooper who had been injured in Sicily a month ago, and was recovering at hospital in London when his heart gave out and he died while listening to the radio two days ago.

Bloody hell, the professor thought. *Bloody, bloody hell.*

"He lived three years longer than his father," a voice behind Tolkien said.

Turning, Tolkien saw that the voice belonged to Eldridge White, the chief of MI6, Britain's foreign intelligence service, to which the professor had twice been attached in the past five years.

"What . . .?" Tolkien said.

"To pay my respects," said White, "and to see you. Shall we walk?"

My dear John,

Please pardon my departure from our regular writing schedule, but last week, while stalking missing documents, a process which you know I have come very much to enjoy, I came across something odd and, I must say, troubling. So troubling that I immediately brought it to the attention of Cardinal Falco, the man in charge of the archives and, I am given to understand, a special and close friend to His Holiness. You will find this hard to believe but I now find myself a prisoner of the Church. I can do my work, but guards follow me wherever I go. My door is locked from the outside at night. I am told it is for my own safety, that, as I am English, and the political situation at the moment so fraught, people will think me a spy. Absurd, of course.

I am also enjoined by the cardinal from speaking about my discovery. Enjoined on the threat of excommunication. Fancy that.

I am an old man and not afraid for my life, but I would like to see an old friend, you, before I die. If you cannot come, I will understand. There is a war on, after all.

My love to Edith and the children.

In Christ,
Fr. Francis
Rome, 15 July 1943

"You intercepted this," Professor Tolkien said, looking up after reading. He and White were sitting on a stone bench under a tree facing a timeworn grave marker enclosed in a low, wrought-iron border fence. He folded Father Morgan's letter and put it in his jacket's inside pocket, next to Robert Gilson's obituary.

"Yes," White replied.

"The others?" Tolkien asked.

"We read them all, of course. But of course so does the Vatican."

"So how did this get through?"

"Your man Morgan gave it to our station chief. It came in the pouch."

"Goodness."

"Yes."

"How did you know I was here?"

"I stopped by the house."

"You're a busy man, Ellie."

White remained silent. He took a moment to look about, as intelligence officers are wont to do. Tolkien followed his gaze. On the cemetery's perimeter road, a small caravan of cars was carrying young Gilson's family and friends back to their lives. Two old men—all the young and most of the middle-aged men were in the war—were filling in the grave. The sun beat down on everything.

A lighthearted remark had crossed Professor Tolkien's mind when he finished Father Morgan's letter. His old guardian, and now good friend, Francis Xavier Morgan, in his mid-eighties, was perhaps getting a bit befuddled in his old age. *Prisoner. Excommunication.* Rather. But then Tolkien remembered that when he last saw Morgan, before he left for Rome in the spring, he was as sound of mind and body as a church bell, the ringing of which got richer and clearer as the years passed. *I am not afraid for my life.*

And then, of course, there was the fact that the chief of MI6, perhaps the busiest and most heavily burdened man in England beside Churchill, had "stopped by" his house in Oxford. Nothing lighthearted about that.

"Who is this Cardinal Falco?" the professor asked.

"That is precisely why I tracked you down," White replied.

"I don't understand."

"You get to the heart of things."

"Shall I go over?" Tolkien asked.

"Yes," White answered, "but I'm afraid I have some bad news."

"Father Morgan's dead."

"Yes. But . . ."

"How did I know?"

"Yes."

"You went to my house, Ellie."

"I thought I should tell you in person, on your own ground."

"Did you tell Edith?"

"No."

Tolkien nodded. Better that this news come from him. "The war?" he asked.

"We're a long way off, old man."

"Does it matter?"

Silence.

"How is your catechism going?" Tolkien asked.

"You know I appreciate our talks."

"I'm afraid I may not be your man anymore."

"John . . ."

During the darkest days of the blitz, in October of 1940, in the midst of fifty-seven straight days of the bombing of London by Hitler's Luftwaffe, White had asked John Tolkien to meet him occasionally, not to talk shop, as it were—which was fine with the professor, since he never considered himself a professional spy, nor an amateur one for that matter—but to talk about Catholicism. White was converting.

"What is your status," Tolkien asked.

"I've done it."

Silence.

"Surely you can say something," said White. "You were an inspiration, after all."

"You're lucky."

"I don't like the sound of that."

"Adult converts never falter."

What a thing to say, Tolkien thought, grimacing inwardly, directing his gaze at the gravestone in front of them. Anywhere but in White's direction. The name on the stone was Theophilus Carter.

"The Gilson boy," said White quietly, sighing almost imperceptibly. "There will, I'm afraid, always be war."

"I thought we fought the war to end all wars."

"We didn't."

"You chose the wrong specimen."

John Tolkien was surprised to see that White, a man steeped in the hard realities of the twentieth century, was embarrassed. Actually he felt this rather than saw it, as the two, both Englishmen to the bone, were studiously avoiding each other's gaze.

"I don't think you're a saint, John," said White. "If that's what you're thinking."

"Neither do I," said Tolkien, a ghost of a smile crossing his face. *Not a saint indeed.* He rose and walked over to Theophilus Carter's grave, to make sure he had read the name right.

"You don't think . . .?" Tolkien said, turning back to face White.

"We had a man watching Morgan," said White. "He was quite healthy for his age, but suddenly he dies in his sleep."

"After learning something deeply troubling."

"And bringing it to this Cardinal Falco."

"Which brings us around to my initial question," said Tolkien. "Who is he?"

"A shadowy figure, a childhood friend of Pacelli's."

"Pius XII."

"Yes. Until recently he was the nuncio to Mussolini's government."

"Nuncio?"

"Ambassador."

"What do you think Father Morgan found?"

"We have people in the Vatican, of course," said White, his eyes now cold and clear, the eyes of a professional. "The rumors are thick. *The pope will make a deal with us; the pope will make a deal with Hitler; Hitler will assassinate the pope and occupy Vatican City.* Outside the white line there is talk that Mussolini will be deposed."

"The white line?"

"The Germans had Mussolini paint a white line around Vatican City. Inside it you are safe, outside you are subject to the fascists' barbaric laws."

Professor Tolkien did not respond. Father Morgan worked in the Vatican Archives Library. A harmless old parish priest, at the end of his usefulness, free to wander about the dark maze that was Vatican City, he might have come across something that was not meant for his eyes, for anyone's eyes.

"He wrote to the pope to get this assignment," Tolkien said.

"Yes, I know."

"They met when Pacelli was in England. Morgan was his confessor here."

"Did Morgan tell you how that came to be?"

"Pacelli walked into the Birmingham Oratory while Father Morgan was preparing for mass. He offered to serve."

"Stooping to conquer."

"Perhaps."

"Why was Pacelli here?"

"He was the papal emissary to the queen's funeral."

"Victoria."

"Yes."

"Extraordinary."

"Yes. Afterward he confessed to Morgan. They became friends, began a correspondence."

"Had I known all this, I would have recruited him."

Tolkien smiled. He could not imagine his old guardian a spy.

"He told me he wanted to end his days in Rome, in the Vatican," said the professor.

"He got his wish, I'm afraid."

"What would you like me to do?"

"Did Morgan know about your extracurricular activities?"

Tolkien did not reply. His operational work for MI6 was supposed to be a secret. MI6 did not officially exist. But once or twice a year he traveled up to Birmingham to visit Father Morgan. And to confess his sins, one or two of which were committed when he was in France in 1940, working for the non-existent White, head of the non-existent MI6. His brow knit. He shrugged.

"Not to worry," said White. "A good thing you did, perhaps."

"What shall I do?"

"Find out what Morgan uncovered, and if it got him killed, for starters."

"For starters?"

"We don't want the pope killed. We don't want him falling in with the Germans. We don't want Italy's Jews slaughtered."

Tolkien, who was walking slowly back to the bench, stopped in mid-stride. "Anything else?" he said. "Climb Everest? Melt the ice cap?"

"See what you can do," said White. He was not smiling. "Let the situation dictate."

"By myself?"

"Your old friend Ian Fleming is going over as well."

"Ah, the plot thickens."

"On another matter, but you'll help him if you can."

"Help him how? What's the assignment?"

"He'll explain. But the thing is, he's . . ."

"He's what?"

"He's erratic."

The professor had not seen Fleming since they visited Albert Einstein in New Jersey in 1940. It would be looked on as an odd thing for an Oxford professor and a vaguely identified admiralty employee to be seen together, so they refrained. There was a cryptic note from time to time, one or two of which seemed too cynical by half to Tolkien. He had been worried about his old colleague and now he understood why. Erratic was not the way an Englishman in the service of his government would want to be described. Unreliable came next, which was a death sentence to a career and a reputation.

"Do you know who Theophilus Carter was?" said Tolkien. He had paused to think and to gaze at the beautiful day before resting his eyes on the Carter gravestone.

"I'm afraid I don't."

"A furniture dealer. Something of an eccentric, if you believe the stories."

"I see."

"You don't."

"No, I don't."

"He was Lewis Carroll's model for The Mad Hatter."

White barked out a short laugh. "I suppose you could say we've gone through the looking glass," he said.

"Worse," said Tolkien. "When do I leave?"

"Tomorrow evening. A car will pick you up at six. You'll go in through Switzerland."

"Flying?"

White's answer was to raise his eyebrows.

"Sorry," said Tolkien. "I puke."

"Yes, I know," said White. "Churchill should have added it to his list."

"His list?"

"Yes, *blood, toil, tears, sweat* . . ."

"I see, and *puke*."

"I'll mention it to him next time I see him."

"Don't. It doesn't work artistically."

Both men smiled, ruefully; the only kind in times of war.

10.
Northern Judea, April 4, AD 60, 7 a.m.

"Why have you taken me here, Father?"

"This land used to belong to my father, your grandfather Jacob."

The young man, Simon's son, Joseph, stood mute.

"Do you know of the sect that call themselves the Nazarenes?"

"Father. . . Yes, I do." Joseph was not surprised by what he perceived as his father's disjointed thought pattern. The old man's hair had turned shockingly white over the past few months, and the blaze in his dark-brown eyes, always intense and often disconcerting, even to his wife and son, had begun to flicker on and off, like a sputtering fire fighting to stay lit. But the mention of his grandfather Jacob was indeed a rare thing. Joseph knew only that he had been unjustly and summarily executed by the Romans, leaving his father to wander alone before he met his mother and could start a new life. His father was looking over Joseph's shoulder now, toward a hill a short distance away. Joseph, eyeing him, saddened but very curious, remained silent.

"Your grandfather was killed on this spot," said Simon.

Both men were bearded and bareheaded; both wore the ankle-length wool *simla* and outer cloak called a *me'il* that men had been wearing in these lands for a thousand years.

Leather sandals protected their feet from the desert's rough surfaces. Both carried walking staffs. Simon pointed his to a barren, sandy spot on the ground that looked like any other for miles in all directions.

"Why have you never spoken of him?" Joseph asked.

"A Roman soldier plunged his sword through his neck into his heart as I watched," said Simon.

Joseph shook his head slightly. "Why have you never told me this?"

"Follow me," said Simon. "I want to show you something."

11.
London, July 18, 1943, 2 p.m.

"Do you know the situation in Rome?"

"No."

"Hitler is there today trying to buck up Il Duce, who's about to be deposed by his own Grand Council. The Allies will be bombing the city tonight and for the next few days. There's talk of the Americans sending in the 82nd Airborne. The Italians want desperately to come over to our side."

"Will we let them?"

"Not likely. They're looking to save face with some kind of conditional surrender."

Ian Fleming remained silent. He was, in fact, familiar with the "situation" in Rome, as MI6 Chief Eldridge White put it, but this was his first invitation to White's office at 54 Broadway, the *sanctum sanctorum* of Great Britain's foreign intelligence service; there was nothing to be gained by appearing to be as in-the-know as old Ellie, who could make or break a career with a nod of the head. Fleming had learned the hard way from his grandfather, Robert Fleming, probably the smartest banker and financier ever to set foot in the city, that boys and young men must never, ever appear to outshine their elders. *Know as much as you like, laddie, but keep it to yourself. No one likes a braggart.*

"The thing is," White continued, "we don't think Herr Hitler will let it happen."

"What will he do?"

"Invade Rome, prop up Il Duce. That's where you come in."

"Sir?"

"Karl Wolff seems to be attracted to one of your spankers."

"They're not all spankers, Sir."

"Certainly not," said White, "but those pictures of Ober-gruppenführer Brauer with those welts on his derrière, well, you know how these things get around."

Fleming winced inwardly at the derision in Ellie White's voice. The chief had never been a fan of the chain of high-class bordellos that he and two other agents had established across southern Europe and North Africa as collection baskets for the information that Axis officers inevitably spewed in the throes of passion. "There's nothing like falling in love with a whore to get the tongue wagging," his fellow agent, Graham Greene, had said, a twinkle in his eye, when they were trying to convince their superiors to authorize Operation Bottoms Up, as the bordello scheme came to be known in the service.

"Who might she be?" Fleming asked.

"Ex-spanker, I should say," said White.

"Some do escape," said Fleming. He was joking. None of his whores were forced to stay in service. But he immediately regretted his attempt at levity. White's craggy face was frighteningly lacking in expression.

"A Signorina Roselli," said the chief. "Ring a bell?"

"Yes, a beauty," said Fleming.

"We think Hitler will put Wolff in charge of Italy. Word has it he's in Rome now making preparations. You see where I'm going?"

"When do I leave?"

"Tonight."

"Cover?" said Fleming. "I'll have to leave the premises to find Claudia."

"There's no time for anything elaborate," White replied. "You'll be attached to our embassy in the Vatican. They'll give you whatever papers you'll need. Be Irish. There are a couple of hundred of them in Rome, trying to do business with Mussolini. Arms, uniforms, rations, liquor, you name it. You speak Italian and German, thank goodness. The Italians don't know the difference between an English and an Irish accent. We've set a couple of our people up as Irish arms dealers and they've done well."

Fleming nodded, enjoying the idea of trying to speak Italian with an Irish brogue.

"How well do you know Miss Roselli?" White asked.

"The usual."

"Is she greedy?"

"Yes."

"There is cash earmarked. A lot of it. We want this to be long lasting. Can you tap her phone?"

"Well, Mussolini runs the phone company. I'll see what I can do."

"He's in trouble. Take advantage of the confusion."

"Yes, Sir."

"There are certain priorities," said White. "You can offer Miss Roselli whatever you wish."

Fleming nodded, trying not to appear too eager. But he was. Besides Operation Bottoms Up, which involved a lot of shagging and little danger, he had been desk bound since his return from his last mission in France some three years earlier. He had spent much of his time learning German and Italian, often practicing on the whores he recruited for Operation Bottoms Up.

"The Italians will want to spirit Mussolini away," the chief continued. "He's a very valuable bargaining chip. The bloodiest war criminal next to Hitler. They'll want to use him to make a better deal for themselves."

"Very sensible."

"Hitler will not want that to happen."

"Also sensible."

"Wolff will be in the middle of it. He's also good friends with Guido Leto, the head of OVRA. Perhaps we can mount an operation if we know where he is."

"I'll speak to Claudia."

"Also," said White, "there is talk that Herr Hitler wants to eliminate the pope, or perhaps kidnap him, bend him to his will. There is some kind of a plot in the works, involving one of Hitler's favorites, a Colonel Otto Skorzeny. We need to prevent that from happening, at all costs."

"It seems," said Fleming, "as though Signorina Roselli will be one of our greatest secret weapons."

"Anything to help turn the tide."

"I thought we were gaining the upper hand?"

"Taking mainland Italy will be a bloody mess. And invading France? It's a long way off."

"What do we know about the Italians' plans for Mussolini, and about the plot to assassinate the pope?"

"Jesus will fill you in."

"Jesus?"

"Our station chief in Rome. J. J.—James Jesus—Pembroke. He's more Catholic than the pope, hence the assignment. You've heard of him?"

"I didn't know that was his middle name."

"Odd family. Both his brothers also bore the middle name 'Jesus.'"

"Bore?"

"Killed in the First War."

"Supposed to end them all, that one."

"It didn't."

No response required here, Fleming thought.

"One more thing," said White.

"Yes, Sir."

"Your friend Professor Tolkien is heading over as well."

"I . . .You don't say? Delighted. Will we be working together?"

"No. He's doing some digging for us involving an old friend of his who died over there."

"I see. Who's the friend?"

"A priest named Morgan."

"Ah, yes, the professor spoke of him when we were in Germany. What happened?"

"We're not sure. It could be nothing, or it could have something to do with Morgan uncovering a dark secret of some kind. He'll be arriving soon after you, reporting to Pembroke."

"Shall I . . .?" said Fleming. There was something in Ellie White's voice that gave him pause. He had heard rumors that White was converting to Catholicism and that Tolkien was his sponsor, if that was the right word.

"I'm worried about him," said White.

"I see," was all Fleming could think of to say. As far as he knew, Ellie White never worried about anyone at ground level, never showed any emotion about anything.

"He's become . . ." said White.

Silencio, Fleming, practicing his Italian, admonished himself. *He's become* what?

"Yes, well," said White. "Tolkien's still an amateur. He's been teaching Beowulf these past years. Keep an eye on him. Give him a hand if you can."

"Of course." Fleming nodded, relieved that White had decided not to suddenly become a human being. *These papists*, he said to himself. *They set too much store by this religion of theirs.*

12.
Northern Judea, April 4, AD 60, 7 a.m.

"What is this?" said Joseph, son of Simon of Scythopolis.

"You know what it is," Simon answered.

The two men were standing, rag torches in hand, in a small, domed cave. Directly in front of them, resting on a shelf cut into the cave's wall, was a roughly made limestone box, perhaps three feet long by two feet wide by two feet high. A crude cross was etched on its front surface. Just above the cross was a roughly cut, one-inch-by-one-inch square opening,

"I don't. Father, please, why have you brought me here?" Joseph had lately become increasingly exasperated with old Simon. He was not slipping into a quiet and passive old age like other men in their circle lucky enough to live into their late fifties and sixties. Last week he had left their house early one morning and not returned until the next evening. *Where have you been, Father? Wandering in the desert. Where did you sleep? In a secret cave.* Now this.

"He had to be buried quickly, you see," said Simon. "The sun was setting."

"Who had to be buried quickly?"

"The Nazarene."

"Father . . ."

"Old Joseph had already purchased the myrrh and aloe."

"Father . . ."

"*Do not interrupt me again.*"

Joseph looked closely at his father, who had, in his remembrance, rarely shown annoyance or irritation, let alone anger. The old man's almond-shaped, dark-brown eyes were now lit not just with anger, but with a fiery light that arrested Joseph in mid-thought. His father's—until this moment always benign—countenance, framed by its white mane, thick, white eyebrows and white beard, now seemed cut from some magnificent stone. He even seemed taller. He had become—the torchlight flickering across his face—one of the prophets he had spoken of so often.

"We soaked the linen and wrapped the body while the women watched," said Simon.

"Father?" said Joseph, who had waited a moment before speaking.

"Yes?"

"May I?"

"Yes."

"The story his followers tell is that Jesus rose bodily into the sky."

"Yes."

"So it is a hoax, as the Romans and the Pharisees say?"

"No."

"But . . ."

"Old Joseph was afraid the council would steal the body. To make a public display of it. To desecrate it. They knew what Jesus had said, that on the third day he would rise. They had heard the Lazarus story." The old man paused and looked at the ossuary. "Joseph, your namesake, told me to take the body away, to bury it properly and to preserve the bones according to my craft."

"And what of the sightings?"

"I was there. I saw him."

"Was it really him, Father?"

70

"Yes."

"Father?"

"Yes?"

"Why are you not then a Christian, a follower of the Nazarene?"

"Because I gave an oath to Joseph of Arimathea to keep the covenant, and to keep these bones, an oath you are going to give to me."

Simon took a yellowing parchment from inside his cloak and handed it to his son. "Old Joseph of Arimathea," said Simon, "predicted that I would sign this when my son took his first breath. And I did. Now you must as well."

The young man took the parchment, quickly scanning to his father's signature scrawled at the bottom.

"You were born and now live because the Christian god wanted it so," said Simon. "You will also have a son. Our line lives and will continue to live because of Jesus of Nazareth. And *for* him."

"Father . . ."

"Sign it," said Simon, "and let me die in peace."

13.
Rome, July 20, 1943, 11 p.m.

Under any other circumstances, Ian Fleming, despite the so-called curfew, would have smoked. Now, however, on enemy soil, the city lit only by a full moon, he quelled his rebellious streak, a streak his depressingly honest mother always modified with the additional adjective "juvenile." He had been standing just inside a dark alley for the past two hours gazing at the front entrance of Via Tasso 145, a brutish-looking gray building that loomed over its working class Lateran neighborhood, a building that Fleming imagined was even more brutish on the inside, containing, as he had been told it did, along with a prison, many of the numerous offices from which Benito Mussolini's henchmen did their work. He had been smoking three or four Morland's Specials per waking hour since he was twenty. Fingering the pack in his jacket pocket, he did some hurried math. *My God*, he thought, *that's a lot of cigarettes.*

Next to the cigarettes was his Ballester-Molina .45, which he had been issued when he arrived yesterday and had trained on for an hour in a converted gymnasium in the bowels of the Vatican, and which he dearly hoped he would not have to use. "It's called the 'Special Ops Executive,'" the Rome station chief, J. J. Pembroke, had told him. "Made in Argentina." Seriously? That's what they called it? Why couldn't they come up with a British-made field pistol? With a different name or, better yet, no name at all? Could the Argentineans, or anyone in South America for that matter, make an automatic pistol that actually worked when called upon? It had misfired twice at the makeshift range yesterday, prompting him to consider turning it upon Pembroke, his training partner, in a leering charade of Russian Roulette. Argentinean Roulette, you might say.

He had reconsidered—no sense killing his boss on his first day in the field in three years—but these dark musings had escalated over the last twenty-four hours, as his search for Claudia Roselli led him nowhere. If he did not find her soon, what would be the point of staying? Ellie White was not a man to waste resources.

It was Pembroke who told him that Herr General Karl Wolff was in town, likely holed up on Via Tasso. "He never fails to *ficken* Claudia when he visits the Eternal City; but be careful," the station chief had said. "It could not be more dangerous out there: Mussolini about to be deposed, the city a cauldron of factions vying to fill the vacuum, the Germans, exasperated with their so-called ally, on the cusp of invasion and occupation." *The devil's playground* is how old JJ had succinctly put it.

Fleming was pondering the various ways he might be able to finesse White into another field assignment when a black Maserati touring car pulled up to the curb next to the alley, and a priest, or at least a man in a priest's getup, got out. The moonlight was so bright that both the man and the car cast a shadow on the uneven, cracked sidewalk. It also revealed the alleged priest's pockmarked face and strangely innocent eyes. A moment later the front door to Via Tasso 145 opened and Claudia Roselli, in a dark trench coat and dark scarf covering her head, stepped out. Fleming watched as Claudia noticed the priest, who beckoned to her to come to him. She didn't.

She stared hard at him for a long moment, then turned back to the building, where she yanked several times at the ornate, brass knob on the thick, front door, each time to no avail. The door had locked itself behind her. Turning, she pointed her middle finger at the priest and headed down Via Tasso, a five-block stretch of nondescript pavement and narrow, broken sidewalk that Fleming knew from his prep work led directly to the rear of St. John Lateran Basilica. She did not seem to be in a hurry but, then again, that was Claudia. Her ass moved to the music of time.

As the priest swung the car door open and was about to get back in, Fleming stepped quickly out of the shadows and struck him on the back of the head with the barrel end of his .45. Down the man-who-would-be-priest went. *That worked OK*, the Englishman said to himself. He reached in and took the key from the Maserati's ignition. Looking up, he saw Claudia turn and look directly at him before rounding a corner. When he got there he saw "Via Statilia" stenciled on a gray building similar to number 145. "Via" was a euphemism. It was an alley, filled with overflowing trash bins, that seemed to lead like a train tunnel into the dark heart of the Lateran section of Rome. No moonlight reached here. The Englishman took a moment to adjust his vision after the relative brightness of Via Tasso to the pitch black of Via Statilia, then quietly stepped in.

Claudia was not in sight, but the visibility being about ten feet, she could have been eleven feet ahead or a hundred. *Bloody hell*, the Englishman thought, *bloody* women. Proceeding cautiously, he caught himself just before stepping into a depression straddled by a plank that was likely hewn in the time of Augustus Caesar. He crossed, keeping his eyes on the plank. Once on the other side he thought, *Is someone in there?* He had heard scurrying. He had been loath to use his pocket torch, but if it was Claudia, well, he would grab her and get the hell away. He shined it and saw rats nibbling on something next to a rusted and pockmarked pipe. He was about to flick off the torch and move on when he heard a muffled grunt in the shadows nearby. Shining the thin beam in that direction he saw, as if in a macabre, stage-lit tableau, Claudia on the ground on her back, and a man bending over her with one hand on her throat and the other raising a knife above his head.

Please work, Fleming said to himself as he drew his Special Ops pistol from his hip and, keeping the torch's diamond-bright beam on the stabber, shot him in the head.

14.
Rome, July 20, 1943, midnight

"I can't believe it's you," said Claudia Roselli.

"It's me," Ian Fleming replied.

"Who was that man?"

"You didn't recognize him?"

"Of course not."

"Start packing," said Fleming.

Claudia, who was sitting on the edge of her bed, stood up and took her time smoothing out her skirt, looking over her shoulder to make sure its rear façade was in order, and taking an extra moment to tuck in and smooth her white silk blouse. All of this dishevelment was the result of her near-death experience in Via Statilia and the hurried trek through the night with her rescuer to her apartment on Via Brunetti in the maze of streets behind the Campo de' Fiori.

"Better?" she asked, staring at Fleming, a thin smile on her lips that she meant to be, if not provocative, at least self-deprecatingly charming. *I'm a mess. Who would want me in this state? You, perhaps, Mr. Fleming?*

"You won't need much," said the Englishman.

Claudia shook her head. Fleming, who had never looked handsomer, his angular British face still slightly flushed from the night's surreal activities, had never played hard to get before, but the night was young, and men were men. She opened the large armoire that stood against one of the bed-room's walls and began extracting things, bending over at the end to pull out a pair of high heels.

"You won't need those," said Fleming.

"I won't stop being a woman, wherever you're taking me. Where is that, by the way?"

"Vatican City."

"You're not serious."

"I am. You're in danger, and I need you. There's no safer place."

"Need me for what?" Claudia leaned down, her left leg bent out, to slip on one of the shoes. She remembered that Fleming loved high heels, the higher the better. After both shoes were on, she began unbuttoning her blouse.

"What are you doing?" Fleming asked.

"Changing. I can't see the pope in these wrinkled clothes."

"You won't be seeing the pope."

"How do you know he's not a client?"

"I need you to work on Karl Wolff," said Fleming, ignor-ing Claudia's flippancy, but not, she noted with satisfaction, the purposefully languid movement of her hands as she undid the last two buttons and slid her long arms out of the shim-mering silk blouse. She was glad she had taken the time before leaving to see Wolff to apply her favorite scarlet nail polish.

"What do you need to know?" she asked, as she reached around to unhook her bra.

"Everything."

"Everything? The size of his wiener schnitzel?"

"You need a new brassiere? My dear Claudia, are you try-ing to seduce me?"

Claudia, smiling, had removed her bra and tossed it on the bed. She knew how beautiful her breasts were and, point-ing them toward Fleming, was now certain that he would momentarily stop playing the professional spy and start play-ing at something else. "*Yes.*"

"Then I'll oblige," said Fleming, stepping to her and taking her face in his hands. "But we don't have much time."

Even Claudia, who had been taken hundreds of ways by hundreds of men, was surprised by what came next. Fleming took his gun from the waistband holster on his right hip and pressed it flat between her breasts. The hard steel against her skin was at first shocking and then exhilarating.

"Put it between your legs," Fleming said.

"What . . .?"

"The safety's on. *Do it.*"

ooooo ooooo ooooo

"How long have you known Karl Wolff?" said Fleming.

"You are a brute," said Claudia. "Un bruto."

Fleming, who was standing over the still-naked Claudia, had quickly re-donned the rough, black, cotton shirt and trousers he had worn for his evening out. "Si," he said, "un bello bruto. How long?"

"I met him a few months ago. One of my Italian clients recommended me."

"Who was that?"

"Edoardo Sica, a member of the Grand Council."

"Good, I may need him."

"For what?"

"Information, Claudia, what else?"

Claudia picked up the Balester-Molina, which lay on the bed next to her. "Shall I shoot you?" she said, pointing it at Fleming.

"Go ahead."

"Where did you learn that trick?" she asked.

"It occurred to me you might enjoy it."

Claudia handed the gun to Fleming, who slipped it into its three-o'clock holster, checking first to make sure the safety was on.

"I did. It was just too . . ."

"Too what?"

"Too fast."

Fleming smiled. "Are you trying to insult me? I told you we didn't have much time. Next time."

"Will there be a next time?"

"If you're a good girl."

"I'll never be a good girl."

"Get dressed," said Fleming. "We have to get to the Vatican while it's still dark, and we have a lot of catching up to do."

While Claudia was dressing, Fleming went into the parlor. Through the open bedroom door, she could see him slightly parting the long drapes that covered the room's one tall window and looking down to the dark street below. *Yes,* she said to herself, *I'm in danger. Someone tried to kill me tonight. Not Falco. He wants to use me. And not Karl Wolff. He needs me to keep seducing Luca Segreto. And I need him, for the money he will pay me when I bring him Luca's secret. The money that will free me from this wretched life.*

PART II

THE PRODIGAL SON

1.
Rome, July 21, 1943, 6 a.m.

"*Here*, you say?" said James Pembroke.

"Yes, I'm afraid so," Ian Fleming replied.

Pembroke and Fleming were sitting in the station chief's windowless, ten-foot-by-ten-foot office, a converted closet in the attic of a squat, stone building that once quartered the officers of the pope's Swiss Guard, but that was abandoned long ago when the roof tiles began to fly away on windy days. Scaffolding, also abandoned, surrounded the building. A single bulb in a wire cage on the ceiling illuminated the room.

"Where?" Pembroke asked.

"Bunking with a nun I've befriended."

"Who, exactly?"

"Her name is Sister Maria Rafaela."

"Security?"

"The nun?"

"No, the whore."

"I gave her something to help her sleep."

"A nun you've befriended? In one day?"

"She sought me out."

"She sought you out? How? She will lead people right to us."

"An underground network of tunnels. She's ninety and knows Vatican City both above and below ground like the back of her hand. She says she was not followed."

"Do you believe her?"

"Lying is a mortal sin, I'm told."

"What did she want?"

"To talk about Father John Morgan. She was helping him do his work. She became attached to him. She thinks he was murdered. Actually she's sure he was murdered. She thinks she knows who killed him, and why."

"What did you tell her?"

"I told her that another agent was coming over to look into Morgan's death, that until he contacted her, she was to cease speaking of her suspicions. It could get her killed as well."

Pembroke nodded. "So now she's guarding your prisoner."

"Yes, though Claudia's not a prisoner."

"So you say. How did you accomplish this in one day?"

"I have a way with women."

"You seduced the nun?"

"She's ninety, and devout. No, I told her I might need help hiding a whore. She seemed intrigued, and agreed."

"What's *her* view of her status? Signorina Roselli's."

"I saved her life for God's sake."

"What happens when she wakes up?"

"She won't for a few more hours."

"What did you give her?"

"Laudanum."

Pembroke nodded again.

"Where is he, by the way?" Fleming said. "Tolkien."

"He arrived late last night. There was a delay in Geneva," the station chief replied. "He'll be a babe in the woods here. No Italian, no German. All these spies running around. Amateurs most of them, even the field people. They're the most dangerous. Keep an eye on him."

Fleming paused before replying. He viewed Professor Tolkien as the hero of their operations in Germany in 1938 and France in 1940. Neither mission would have been successful without Tolkien's courage and intelligence.

"You'd be surprised at how well Professor Tolkien can take care of himself," he said, finally. *Babe in the woods, indeed.*

"I admire your loyalty," said Pembroke, "but C mentioned his concerns to me, which I felt he wanted me to pass on."

Fleming nodded. "Understood," he said, though he didn't. *What was going on with old John Ronald?*

"Do you know there are zones in the Vatican?" Pembroke asked, breaking into Fleming's thoughts.

"Zones?"

"English, American, Italian, even German."

"I must say, I'm a bit confused."

"France, Britain, Italy, Belgium, Germany and Poland have resident ambassadors. The others are a bit in the shadows."

"But they're here."

"Yes, in full force. Just about every country in Europe and South America; even a few in Asia. The place is teeming with spies of every stripe, color and creed, each with his own dubious agenda. And they each have their own space. The Vatican is a labyrinth. A hundred-and-nine-acre labyrinth. Certain parts are known to certain people, but the whole is known to no one."

"I say, *our* agenda isn't dubious? Or is it?" *I'll make this chap smile if it kills me,* Fleming said to himself.

"We're the exception," Pembroke replied, expressionless, "and the Americans."

"And this relates to our Signorina Roselli how?"

"The OSS has finally arrived. Their quarters are in the basement of the train station."

"The Vatican has a train station?"

"Yes, rarely used. When Claudia Roselli wakes up, take her and Sister Rafaela there. There's a tunnel from our quarters here to the station. Sister probably knows it."

"The good sister too?"

"Yes. We need to keep them to ourselves for a while."

"Why?"

"The priest you knocked over was Father Carlo Fiore. Your description matches him exactly. He works for a cardinal named Federico Falco. The Hawk. He's the head of Vatican intelligence. If Falco wants her, we want her first."

"I think she knows Falco wants her," Fleming said.

"Is that what she told you?"

"Yes," said Fleming. "She's been in hiding."

"But she ventured out to see Wolff?"

"Yes. She's a whore. He pays her well. She has to eat."

"What's Falco's interest?"

"She refused to say, and I didn't press her," Fleming answered. "I was in a hurry to get her under control. I will get it out of her later. What is Mussolini's status? I'd like to get Claudia back into bed with Wolff as soon as possible."

"We're not sure. The Fascist Council is wrangling. They have to do something to try to save the country from ruin, and all bets are they'll depose Il Duce, imprison him and sue for peace, but it could be tomorrow, it could be next week or next month."

"We've landed on the mainland," said Fleming. "That should make them nervous."

"I'm sure it does, but it will be months before we get close to Rome. In the meantime, something else has come up."

"Something else?"

"Yes."

"More important than a direct line to Hitler's chief of operations in Italy? To information that will help me kidnap Mussolini out from under the Italians and the Germans?" Fleming did not mind changing missions in midstream, or having two missions going forward at the same time. He just rather liked the idea of putting a leash on Claudia Roselli, figuratively speaking of course.

"No," Pembroke replied. "But it's very intriguing. We've been approached by someone who says he knows who wants Claudia dead, and why. He wants to make a deal."

"Who?"

"No name yet."

"Who approached you?"

"An intermediary. A rabbi."

"A rabbi? Are there any non-clerical spies in Rome?"

"Yes, a rabbi," said Pembroke. He was not smiling.

"Why us?" Fleming asked.

"He says he has information that is so important, we'll pay any price."

"The Americans have a lot more money than we do."

"They weren't here until yesterday."

"What's his price?"

"Evacuate Rome's Jews."

Fleming looked at Pembroke, whose face remained expressionless.

"How many are there?" Fleming asked.

"I'm told fifteen thousand."

"*Claudia*? I say . . ."

"Did you debrief her?"

"There was nothing to . . ."

"She spent the evening with Karl Wolff."

"Yes, of course, but that was before I told her what her mission would be. She pumped him, but . . . well, I daresay . . ." Fleming, smiling ruefully, stopped in mid-sentence, not because he did not like to appear to be crude—he loved double *entendres*—but because of the continued grim set of Pembroke's rather handsome face. *Stubborn chap*, he thought.

"Yes, I take your point," Pembroke replied.

"She's interested, naturally," said Fleming. "I was about to tell you her asking price."

"Claudia knows something *already*," Pembroke said. "Something she discovered God knows where and God knows from whom. Find out what it is and if she revealed it to Wolff. Or anyone else for that matter. In the meantime, she doesn't leave the American zone, and neither does your Sister Rafaela."

Fleming nodded. "I'm a bit confused," he said. "You know I left Eton and Sandhurst early, a slow learner. How does the rabbi know about Claudia and her supposed secret? And how does he know who wants her dead?"

"He didn't say, only that his principal knows."

"But you believe him."

"Yes. Falco is looking for her, and someone tried to kill her. I'd say she knows something important."

"It could have been a jealous lover I shot last night."

"And Fiore?"

"Another jealous lover."

"Stop it, Fleming."

"Sorry. Speaking of that dead fellow, what is the status of my pictures? I do hope that new gadget worked. Ingenious what those chaps at Bletchley Park are doing."

"We can't trust any photo lab in Rome. The film will go in the 7 a.m. pouch to London. One more thing."

"Yes?"

"Morgan uncovered something and he ends up dead. The whore probably whispered something in someone's ear and she's nearly killed."

"The whore and the priest," said Fleming. "Maybe they have the same secret."

"My point," said Pembroke, "is that C wants to know what these secrets are. Do you know what that means?"

"Yes," Fleming answered. "Tolkien and I don't leave Rome without them."

"Correct. Now that you have confidence in your Ballester-Molina, you should be fine."

Fleming's eyes narrowed. *Was that a joke? Is he sending me up?*

Pembroke was not smiling, but there was a slight gleam in his eye.

By God, he is, Fleming thought. *He's human.*

2.
The Villa Segreto, July 21, 1943, 7 a.m.

Luca Segreto buttoned his shirt at the tall window of his bedroom, looking down at the prophet Moses reincarnated in a business suit: his father, Pietro—his hair white and unruly, his eyebrows—just as white and bushy—protruding over dark, burning eyes, eyes lit from within by something only he saw. The face of God perhaps. Pietro was sitting listening intently to a wireless radio resting on a wrought-iron table. Behind him, in the shadow of the Segreto mansion, his hands clasped behind his back, stood a frail, balding, birdlike man: Old Silvano, the only name Luca had ever known or used for the eighty-year-old retainer who had served Pietro for most of his life. On the table next to the radio was a china espresso cup with a silver spoon resting on its saucer, and a small, silver pill box. Keeping his attention on the radio, his head never moving, Moses reached for the pill box, removed its lid and placed a portion of its contents under his tongue. He then turned and nodded to Silvano, who, quite spryly for a man his age, stepped forward, took the pill box, and retreated into the house.

The wide stone patio that extended from the rear of the stately old villa on the Appian Way, the villa that eight generations of Segretos had owned and inhabited for the past two hundred years, was in shade, but the morning sun, rising on the opposite side of the house, drenched the lawn and tennis court and surrounding gardens that lay beyond the patio in golden light. *So this is what 7 a.m. looks like*, Luca said to himself, smiling. *Papa, you have shown me something new and exciting.*

But of course he would not say such a thing to the stern old man sitting below. There was no teasing in what was left of the Segreto family living in their crumbling mansion on two hundred overgrown acres just a few kilometers beyond Rome's old southern gate. He wondered why he had been summoned. Could it have something to do with the crazy story old Pietro had told him last week, and the oath he had had him take? *The bones of Christ*—my God, the old man was *pazzo*, off his nut, as his American friends would say. He missed those friends, from his boarding school days in Switzerland. The war had put an end to all that. Now he ran occasional errands for the manager of his father's private bank during the day, and drank and partied at night in the basement clubs and cheap bars that catered to the students and hangers-on from Sapienza University in San Lorenzo, a seedy, Roman neighborhood only fifteen minutes away in Luca's two-seater Alfa Romeo.

That is, that was what he did at night until he met Claudia Roselli. My God, *Claudia*. He got dizzy just thinking about her. *Where are you, Claudia? Why haven't you answered your phone?*

His shirt buttoned, Luca was about to turn away, to go down to hear whatever pronouncement Moses was about to make, when Silvano reappeared on the terrace. Standing next to him was a priest with a pockmarked face and a bright white bandage around his head. Pietro nodded and Silvano stepped back into the shadows while the priest approached Moses. Luca's beautiful hazel eyes widened as old Pietro extended his right hand to the priest, who, reaching the old man, bent and kissed his ring, then straightened and waited to be invited to sit.

3.
Rome, July 21, 1943, 7 a.m.

"Is this what you wanted me to see?" asked Professor John Tolkien.

The Englishman had removed the top of the cracked and musty portfolio that Sister Rafaela had retrieved from its hiding place and laid on the scarred trestle table before him. He was shining the miniature torch/camera that his friend and colleague Ian Fleming had loaned him onto the top document.

"Yes," replied Sister Maria Rafaela. "But you must be quick."

"I don't read Italian."

"They are in Latin."

"It's not any Latin that I'm familiar with."

Using Fleming's ingenious and highly practical little device, the professor illuminated and virtually simultaneously photographed each document in the old case, turning each carefully over to make sure he captured whatever might be on the back. Most were letters. Some looked like official decrees. Dust from the two-hundred-year-old paper rose and swirled gently around them as he worked—the subterranean chamber that Sister had brought him to was as dark and still and lifeless as a tomb—while the dried and crumbling wax that once held the impressions of official seals fell onto the table. These Sister Rafaela swept with her right hand into a voluminous pocket on the front of her habit. Her hands, bony, gnarled, and spotted, moved swiftly and with purpose.

Professor Tolkien took a moment to read the last document after he photographed it. This was in traditional Latin that he indeed could read:

> On him, Archbishop Patricio Benedetti, we decree the sentence of excommunication, of anathema, of our perpetual condemnation and interdict; of privation of dignities, honors, and property on him and his descendants, and of declared unfitness for such possessions; of the confiscation of his goods and of the crime of treason; and these and the other sentences, censures and punishments which are inflicted by canon law on heretics and are set out in our aforesaid missive, we decree to have fallen on this man to his damnation.
>
> Clement XII, Episcopus Servus Servorem Dei

"Hurry," said Sister Rafaela.

"Done," Tolkien said, replacing the portfolio cover. "Are there other portfolios like this?" he asked.

"No, but there are documents missing from this one."

"What documents?"

"Old letters on parchment, written in Aramaic. And something from 1939, with the papal seal, and the signature of Pius XII. I saw them when Father Morgan went through this portfolio."

"Where are they?"

"I don't know. Perhaps Cardinal Falco took them."

"Why would he?"

"Father Morgan brought several of the documents from this book to Cardinal Falco. Letters from 1735 from the

Archbishop of Constantinople. Two nights later he died in his sleep."

"Did Father Morgan tell you what was in those letters?"

"The bones of Christ."

"What?"

"They speak of the bones of Christ."

Impossible, Tolkien said to himself, but he forged ahead. "Did Father Morgan speak of a Bishop Benedetti who was excommunicated?" he asked.

"Yes. He said that Bishop Benedetti had discovered the existence of the bones, and of a key to the ossuary that held them, a key buried with children."

"Are there children buried in Vatican City?"

"Yes."

"Can you show me where?"

"Yes, but not now. Now we must go. Cardinal Falco has eyes everywhere."

"Does he know about your maze of tunnels?"

"I don't know. I hope not, but he is not called the Hawk for nothing. He flies high above and sees the smallest movement."

"How long have you been working here, Sister?"

"Seventy years."

Tolkien was speechless. *Seventy years.*

"I had a child out of wedlock and gave her up," the nun said, "and then joined my order. I was eighteen. I was assigned here after I took my vows because I was thought unfit to do anything else. I had worked in a bordello, you see."

"Worked in a bordello. I . . ."

"Don't speak. I have loved my life, and loved Christ."

Tolkien looked carefully at the frail old woman standing next to him. Her skin was just parchment over bones, her weight less than a child of ten, the wrinkles on her face a web spun over a long life. But her dark eyes were bright, shining with something the Englishman had not seen in a while. Utter devotion. He remembered that look in his mother's eyes, there until the day she died.

"We must get back," said Sister Rafaela, interrupting Tolkien's thoughts. "Your colleague left someone in my charge. A prostitute, from the looks of her. She will be waking soon."

"How do you know she's a prostitute?"

"The costumes change," Sister said. "But not the sadness."

"I . . ."

"We must go."

4.
Rome, July 21, 1943, 10 a.m.

Karl Wolff was not a man to miss the main chance in life. He had thus risen to be second-in-command to SS Chief Heinrich Himmler, the second most powerful, and therefore feared, man in Germany, and widely known to be Hitler's handpicked successor; and he was now about to be in charge of all of Italy, a command putting him on a par with Jodl and Keitel, real soldiers who were respected by the Führer and revered by the German people. Gazing down at the documents that Claudia Roselli had handed him four days ago, Wolff knew that his greatest accomplishment was at hand. He would turn the tide of the war in Germany's favor. The result would be either complete victory or a stalemate from which the Fatherland would emerge intact and very powerful.

But he had to be careful, very careful. Only yesterday he had told Hitler to his face that he would be happy to kidnap the pope, that he would have a plan on the great leader's desk within a week. This was, of course, insane. The world's Catholics would turn on Germany with a vengeance, a turn of events that Hitler seemed blind to, but that Wolff knew would be disastrous and would guarantee the destruction of his beloved country.

Sitting across from him at his desk at Via Tasso was Otto Skorzeny, an SS officer, just promoted by Himmler himself to the rank of *Standartenführer*, the equivalent of a full Wehrmacht colonel. At the age of thirty-five Skorzeny had already had a meteoric career. Wounded on the Eastern Front, recipient of the Iron Cross—only given for bravery under fire—he had been recently appointed commander of the SS unit *Friedenthal*, which would be responsible for developing and executing all German guerilla and infiltration warfare in all theatres. Hitler, Wolff had been told, loved him like a son. Nevertheless, Skorzeny, and thus Hitler, would have to be lied to. Manipulated and lied to.

"Otto," Wolff said, "is that scar on your cheek from Russia?"

"No, it is a *schmiss*."

"Ah, you were a fencer."

"*Ja*."

"I have two other assignments for you."

"I am here for one purpose. As you know."

Ah, thought Wolff, *throwing his weight around already. Sent here by the Führer himself. Handpicked.*

"The situation here is quite volatile," Wolff replied, a grave look on his handsome, square-jawed Aryan face. "The Allies have landed on the Italian mainland. We are all pushing ourselves to the limit and beyond. I know how important the kidnapping of the pope is. I spoke just yesterday with the Führer. But can you and your men plan and execute more than one mission at a time?"

"That depends on the missions."

"What is your unit strength?"

"One hundred men."

"Including officers?"

"I am the only officer. Ten are *Unteroffizieres*."

"How many men will you need to extract the high priest?"

"I don't know yet. Perhaps ten."

"You can't storm the place of course."

"Why not?"

Why not indeed? thought Wolff. *This is a beast with no fear. No wonder Hitler loves him like a son. An adopted son of course, the Führer's sexuality being non-existent. Better not to give him a direct order just yet.*

"Present me with a plan within three days."

"*Jawohl.*"

"And two other plans."

"*Jawohl.*"

"One involves our friend Mussolini. He is going to be deposed very soon. We are concerned the Italians will hide him away. Be prepared to prevent that, or to retrieve him."

"*Jawohl.*"

"The second involves a story I heard recently. The source is a whore named Claudia Roselli. She says that a family of Jews in Rome has been hiding Christ's bones for two thousand years. She asked me for a large sum of money to tell me who this family is."

For the first time in the interview Skorzeny revealed, by a slight lifting of the eyebrows, something of what he might be thinking. "Are you Catholic?" Wolff asked.

"I was, but no longer."

"Then you're not."

"I agree." The subject of religion was a touchy one among the Nazis. No one knew this better than Wolff, who, as Himmler's aide-de-camp before the war, had been tasked with developing a set of rituals for supplicating the sculptured SS god, Wralda. Insane of course, but no good Nazi could be a traditional Christian, let alone Catholic, and survive. The party, the state, were all, and everyone knew it. The rest was all nonsense made up by Himmler to indulge his fantasies about naked men.

"If what Signorina Roselli says is true," said Wolff, "you realize what it means."

"What does it mean?"

"We can destroy Catholicism, undermine the Church, take away all of the pope's power."

"What power does he have? He has no army."

"I see you have read Comrade Stalin's speeches."

"Stalin?" Wolff noted the suspicious look on Skorzeny's scarred face. Hitler hated Stalin and anything that Hitler hated all Germans were naturally supposed to hate.

"It's not important," the general said. "I'm talking about moral power. The pope of Rome has five hundred million devout followers." Moral power would, Wolff knew, be a term foreign to Otto, but no matter. He could probably tease out its meaning if he put his dull mind to it.

"I see."

"We can put the Church out of business if we find these bones. Christ was supposed to have risen bodily into heaven. Finding his bones will debunk the whole story."

"How will I find the whore?" Skorzeny asked.

"She lives in Rome, near the Campo de' Fiori. She is waiting for my call. My assistant will give you her number."

"Am I to pay her?"

"No, get the name of the family then kill her."

"*Jawohl.*"

ooooo ooooo ooooo

After Skorzeny left, Wolff picked up the phone on his desk and dialed a four-digit number. A phone on the other end rang twice and the German general hung up. Within seconds his phone rang.

"Guido," Wolff said, picking it up.

"Si."

"Has your king summoned the great oaf?"

"Not yet."

"He is waiting for what, exactly?"

"For Badoglio to secure enough votes in the Grand Council."

"How is that coming along?"

"He is close."

"My plans have changed."

"In what way?"

"Let them take him away."

"But . . ."

"We can find him later."

Silence. Wolff knew what Guido Leto was thinking. "Don't worry, my old friend," he said. "We will still be in charge. You will still be the head of OVRA. I just need to create a diversion."

"He will be hard to find."

"I have just the man for the job."

"Who?"

"Colonel Otto Skorzeny. We will have dinner soon and I will introduce you."

"As you wish."

"In the meantime, I have another favor to ask."

"*Certo.*"

5.
Rome, July 21, 1943, 11 a.m.

The orphanage in the Trastavere neighborhood of Rome where Claudia Roselli was born and raised was officially called the Ospizio Apostolico di San Michele, but in the girls' dorm it was La Casa di Topolino Della Vergogna, loosely translated as "Mickey's House of Shame." This was one of the reasons why being a prostitute was so easy for Claudia. The nuns there never ceased to remind her that she was born out of wedlock, that, as a result, though she had achieved this terrible status through no fault of her own, she had a special mission from Jesus and his Blessed Mother to be pure, to lead an exemplary life. She had been chosen, they said. Some were well intentioned. They believed that purity of body led to paradise; but most were resentful hags, young and old.

Despite her bad history with nuns, she regretted having drugged sweet old Sister Rafaela, stripping her down to her underskirts and stealing her tunic, coif and veil. *That* was probably a sin. But God did not seem angry with her. He had placed a kindly seminarian in her way, who led her on her "mission of mercy" to a little-used door on the Vatican's southern wall, where, he said, she would see a lovely path that would take her along the Tiber to her destination. She would not have done these things as, despite her profession, she considered herself a Catholic, albeit in absentia, nor would she have returned to Mickey's House of Shame for the world, but her options were very limited. Cardinal Falco's agents had been following her for days and would surely be watching her apartment. Why the Hawk had tried to kill her—and why the handsome Englishman had intervened—was not hard to figure out. *The bones of Christ must truly exist.*

There was, of course, a church on the grounds of the orphanage, the church of Santa Maria del Buon Viaggio, five hundred years old and in serious disrepair. Even when Claudia was resident it was little used, the parish priest and Mickey's nuns preferring the small chapel in the main *ozpizio* for their daily mass. It seemed now to be abandoned completely. The massive front door could not be budged, but the smaller entrance on the side swung open easily enough. She had not expected Luca to get there before her, but there he was, eager boy, sitting in a front pew.

How extremely happy he had been to hear from her.

"Anything," he had answered when she told him she had a favor to ask.

6.
Rome, July 21, 1943, noon

"Escaped, you say?" said John Tolkien.

"Yes. Gone," Ian Fleming replied.

"How?"

"She drugged Sister Rafaela and stole her habit."

"I thought you drugged *her*."

"It seems I didn't give her enough."

"Any sign of her?"

"I've been poking into corners and asking discreet questions, but no luck. She must have gone outside."

"Is Sister all right?"

"She has a headache, but otherwise yes."

"What happened?"

"When Sister returned from her excursion with you this morning, Claudia had brewed tea."

The two men were sitting in camp chairs on the roof above the small suite of offices that housed the British Embassy to the Vatican. To the east the Tiber meandered south. On the river's far bank the bronze statue of St. Michael, sheathing his sword atop Castel Sant'Angelo, glistened in the midday sun. Below them, spread out like a miniature medieval village in a child's model train set, was the whole of the enclave which held within its walls more power and wealth than many countries on earth.

"What now?" Tolkien asked.

"I'll have to find her."

"You don't seem too concerned."

"I am, but it may be for the best. She's hiding something, and may lead us to it, or at least to some interesting people."

"Where will you start?"

"The other whores might know where she'd be likely to hole up."

"The other whores?"

"I run a brothel in Rome. Claudia worked there for a few months when she returned from Athens."

"Goodness."

"MI6 is in the prostitution business," said Fleming. "I set it up, recruited the worker bees, and now oversee the thing, as well as similar operations in Athens and Alexandria, from London. I recruited Claudia in Athens."

"Why?"

"Nazi and fascist pillow talk."

"Pillow talk?"

"Information gathered from men of power in the throes of lust."

"Oh my. I . . ."

"I'm not proud of it."

"No need to apologize."

"It's what I've been doing since we parted last."

"Three years? They're wasting your talents."

Fleming cleared his throat. If forced to, he would admit to himself that he was a little afraid of the good professor. That was it, really. Tolkien was good, and he, Ian Lancaster Fleming, was bad. He could almost hear him saying, *You lack discipline, Ian,* something his father had said to him once when he was seven, an offhand remark that, as fate would have it, he had never forgotten. What had he done to merit that remark? He couldn't remember exactly. Something to do with strawberry jam all over his hands and face and a broken jar on the floor.

"I may have overstepped my bounds," Fleming said at length, his throat cleared, and no more delaying tactics to hand, "in courting the wife of a certain member of parliament."

"You're your own worst enemy."

"My mother's sentiments as well."

"Speaking of finding Signorina Roselli," Tolkien said, "I'm told there's a white line you can't cross."

"Correct," Fleming replied.

"How serious is it?"

"Why? Are you thinking of doing some sightseeing?" Fleming smiled his charming smile as he said this, taking a drag on his seventh post-breakfast Morland's Special, blowing the smoke into the clear Italian air.

"No, of course not."

"This place is only a hundred acres or so," said Fleming. "For now the Italians patrol it, but, well, they're Italian these Italians, and this is their Church, so they are *apatico*, half-hearted, about it. When the Germans arrive, there will be armored jeeps around the clock; snipers and lookouts in surrounding buildings. *They* will be serious."

"Why?"

"It is not the Führer's Church. In fact, he hates it. But he is forced to concede that the Vatican is a country unto itself, a strictly *neutral* country, with diplomatic relationships all over the world. The embassies are, of course, filled with spies, enemies of the Reich."

"What about the pouch? Ambassadors traveling home?"

"They can travel a specific route to and from Ciampino."

"Does Pembroke know?"

"About Claudia?"

"Yes. That she's escaped."

"No. I hope to have her back before very long."

"How long does this pouch business take?" Tolkien asked.

"We should have something by late tonight. Why? What do you think you found?"

"A bishop was blackmailing the pope. Two hundred years ago."

"Over what?"

"Something to do with Christ's remains."

"I thought there *were* no remains," said Fleming. "That was the whole point. Of the magic, I mean."

"Catholics don't look on it as magic."

"I know they don't. Poor choice of words. So this may be what got your Father Morgan killed. I can understand why."

"It's starting to look that way," said Tolkien. "There's a cardinal here named Falco who's had what he thinks were the last of the documents destroyed. Sister Rafaela saved a few. The pouch will tell us more."

"Pembroke tells me Falco is the head of Vatican intelligence."

"Yes," said the professor, "he briefed me as well. What did *you* send?"

"Pictures of the man I shot last night. They have thousands of photos on file at Bletchley Park."

"You think they may find a match?"

"Not very likely, but it's worth the effort."

"So you're going out to your brothel. What about the white line?"

"Pembroke's people have shown me a couple of secret ins and outs. I have papers. I've forced myself to learn Italian and German over the last three years. Too much time on my hands. I'll be fine. What will you do? Until the pouch comes back."

"I'm thinking of seeing the pope."

"The pope? Are you serious?"

"Father Morgan was his confessor years ago in England."

"I see."

"No you don't," said Tolkien. "But believe me, it's quite a special relationship, priest to priest, as you can imagine. And when the penitent becomes the pope of Rome, well . . ."

"*Can* you, actually?"

"Probably not, but I'm going to try."

"What will you discuss?"

"Our mutual friend, Father Morgan."

"There's something to be said for going right to the top. Of course this Cardinal Falco fellow might be an obstacle. He may have . . ."

"He *may have* what?"

"Killed Morgan," Fleming replied, "not to put too fine a point on it."

Professor Tolkien smiled the rueful smile of someone who has realized he may have made a mistake, a mistake on a fairly grand scale. He had never had any illusions about the men who populated the clergy. They were men, after all. They sinned. The Church itself, however, was a different matter. It was an idea that had endured for two thousand years. If it were proven to be a false idea, well, better to learn sooner rather than later. Perhaps such a lesson would confirm the doubts that had plagued him lately. As if to punctuate this rather appalling thought, he heard a low rumble in the distance to the north. *God is clearing his throat*, he thought, smiling even more ruefully, *about to reprimand me.*

Both men turned to look out over the parapet in the direction of the rumbling noise, which was growing louder by the second.

"Do you hear that?" said Tolkien.

"Aircraft," said Fleming. "American B-17s. Flying Fortresses."

A few moments later the first of a series of v-shaped bomber squadrons appeared over the northwest quadrant of the city. The lead squadron dipped and the others followed, fanning out left and right. Suddenly a curtain of bombs was falling and the structures below beginning to burst into flames.

"What's over there?" Tolkien asked.

"San Lorenzo," said Fleming. "Freight yards, steel factories. My brothel."

"Your brothel?"

"Yes."

"Let's hope . . ."

"A prayer would be better," said Fleming. "I need live whores right now if I'm to find Claudia."

"There's no opposition," said Tolkien.

"The Italians are done."

"They helped Hitler in the Blitz," said the professor. "I saw their planes."

"I saw them too," Fleming replied. "The fools."

They watched as the bombers banked en masse and headed home, leaving hundreds of burning buildings and huge billows of black smoke in their wake.

7.
Rome, July 21, 1943, noon

The first thing Ian Fleming noticed as he stepped onto a slippery stone dock was the acrid smell in the air. As the launch was approaching its destination, he thought the humid night had suddenly turned pungently foggy, but now he realized it was residual smoke from the bomb raid that his boatman had made his way through as they entered the calm waters of the San Lorenzo district. His eyes burning, he looked up and managed to pick the warehouse that housed MI6's Roman brothel out of the darkness. A squat, two-story affair, thoroughly blacked out, it rose in the night sky directly above him perhaps fifty feet from the river's edge. *Closed*, he thought. *Good decision. Bombed while shagging not quite the thing. Must compliment the madam.*

The two-hour ride north up the looping Tiber and its tributary, the Paglia, with the launch's running lights off and at five knots per hour, had been slow and monotonous. He had talked to himself in this slightly mad vein the entire time. "Silenzio," his boatman, Giuseppe, had said at the outset, and then not another word. "Attendere," Fleming said now, his face grim. *Hell of a conversation*, Fleming thought, *tremendously stimulating.*

Looking again at the warehouse, the Englishman now saw a sliver of dim light at the bottom of a first floor window.

Sloppy, he thought, and then the light went out. He had intended on entering the building unannounced through the back door. He had a key. But that on-and-off sliver of light bothered him. He stepped onto dry land and in two seconds was flat against the warehouse's rear wall. He crept along the building's perimeter like an upright crab until he reached a point where he could peer around a corner to the street in front. Parked at the curb directly opposite the building's decidedly unprepossessing front door was a German flag car. A Wehrmacht soldier, a grizzled veteran by the look of him, was leaning against the Daimler's fender, smoking.

"You can trust him," Pembroke had said of Giuseppe. "He was in the Italian Navy before he became a monk. He hates Mussolini, and Hitler." *I hope so*, Fleming said to himself, as he eyed the German soldier. *I may be a while.*

8.
Rome, July 21, 1943, 11 p.m.

"I don't remember," said Luca Segreto.

"You had had too much wine," Claudia Roselli replied.

"You drugged me," said Luca.

For a moment Claudia did not reply. She did not reveal her shock, but she felt it. Was he smarter than she gave him credit for? Did he fake that slurred speech? She paused to collect her thoughts, but only for a moment. She knew that silence was easy to misread, especially by insecure young men, which meant virtually all young men.

"Drugged you?" she said, frowning. *How can you offend me so?*

"Your body," Luca answered. "Your pussy."

"Ah," Claudia said, turning her frown into a warm, coy smile. A little wide-eyed innocence went a long way with some men. "Flattery will get you everywhere."

"But I honestly don't remember."

Claudia, her feet back under her, again paused. The information she needed from Luca was no longer just about making her rich. It was now about saving her life as well. The bed they were lying in was just a mattress on a weathered plank floor, which she could feel under her, and which, strangely, reminded her of playing make-believe games with her housemates at St. Michael's. Outside, she could hear the lake lapping

113

against the boathouse's cypress walls. She decided to change the subject. She believed him when he said he didn't know where the ossuary was, and that he didn't even remember telling her about it in the first place. She took it as an opportunity for a fresh start.

"Are you sure we won't be discovered here?" she said.

"Yes, I'm sure."

"It can't be seen from the house?"

"No, we are completely hidden."

"What about the groundskeeper? The servants?"

"There is no groundskeeper and only one servant."

"Does he come out here?"

"Old Silvano?" Luca smiled; a smile that was so innocent and disarming that it stopped Claudia's heart for a fraction of a second. "He is my friend. He knows I come to the boathouse," Luca continued, "when I am in hiding from my farther. He will bring us food and keep our secret."

"Will he fix the roof?" Claudia asked archly, a faux frown on her beautiful face.

A steady light rain had been falling when they arrived and they had had to move the mattress to a dry corner of the room.

"No, he has been told to let the boathouse fall to pieces."

"Why?"

"My father ordered it when my brother left."

"You have a brother?"

"He sailed on the lake. He ran away fifteen years ago. We think he's dead."

"Why dead?"

"Or in America."

"What happened?"

"He had a fight with my father and ran away."

"Over what?"

"I don't know. I was four at the time. My father doesn't talk about him."

114

"Your father still has *you.*"

"He thinks I am a wastrel."

"Are you?"

"Yes."

Claudia had expected Luca to smile when he answered, or at least assume a look of faux indignation, but he did neither. She found herself missing his smile, which was dazzling, and wondering where this serious Luca had come from.

"Better," she said, "to have a broken family than none at all, like me."

"I will be your family."

You are a fool as well as a wastrel, Claudia said to herself, remembering Luca's whispered "marry me" just before he climaxed a few minutes ago. *But perhaps, dear Luca, I* will *marry you, as long as you inherit your father's money. Perhaps I don't have to discover the whereabouts of this crazy, blasphemous ossuary after all.*

"I meant it," Luca said. "Marry me. You think me young and foolish, but no one will ever love you as I do."

"Young men say a lot of things in the heat of the moment," said Claudia. *How did he know what I was thinking?* she asked herself. *Strange boy.*

"I came when you called," said Luca.

"And I am grateful."

"I can pass any test."

"Luca?"

"Yes?"

"Your father must be very rich if he owns a bank."

"He's transferred the bank to a gentile friend."

"Transferred the bank? Why?"

"The racial laws of 1938. My father knew they were coming. Jews would not be allowed to own large businesses. He signed it over in 1937. He still controls it, but sooner or later the government will seize its assets and shut it down. Anything connected with Jews is under constant surveillance, especially a bank. OVRA has paid informers everywhere. A teller will turn him in, or an accountant, or a postman."

"He must still have his own money."

"He's given most of it away."

"Given it away?"

"To pay for Jews to escape."

"From Italy? I thought they were safe here. Are you sure?"

"Italy, France, Holland. Yes I'm sure. Whoever asks for help, he gives it."

"You have a strange family."

"There is no family, just me and my father."

"How long can I stay?"

"As long as you wish."

Claudia stroked Luca's chest, then ran her fingers down his stomach and abdomen and rested them on his pubic hair, which, though a bit more curly, was as black and silky as the long tresses covering his Apollo-like head. "Your family," she said when she saw that he was starting to get aroused, "has kept the bones of Christ for two thousand years. Your father made you take an oath."

"So you say."

"So *you* said. Is it true?"

Luca, naked, rose from the mattress and walked over to the open window that looked out over the lake. *David*, Claudia thought, looking at his rounded ass, and remembering his beautiful frontal equipment: the cock, the balls, the *body* of a Michelangelo creation. And the face of an emperor. A Julius Caesar. The brain, though, what was in it?

"I don't know if it's true," Luca said, turning to face Claudia, and tapping his right forefinger against his temple. "My father may be getting *incrinato in testa*."

"I think it's true," said Claudia.

"Why?" Luca had returned to the mattress and was sitting at its edge wiping his feet with a towel. The rain had stopped while they made love, but there were scattered puddles on the boathouse's wooden floor.

"I told Cardinal Falco," Claudia replied. "It was he who tried to kill me."

"Claudia . . ."

"It's true."

"Who is Cardinal Falco?"

"A Vatican *pezzonovante,* one of the princes of a great aristocratic family. He pays me for information."

"Is that all he pays you for?"

"Yes." The boy had put his question in the present tense, but she would have lied no matter how he phrased it, or what tense he put it in. Sexual jealously was a useful tool, but one to be underused, especially with someone like Luca Segreto, who really believed he loved her. Neither she nor he knew yet the limits of his passion, nor of his anger, if it were ever to be aroused.

"How do you know it was him?" Luca asked.

"His assistant has been following me."

"Who is that?"

"Carlo Fiore, a priest with a pockmarked face."

9.
Rome, July 21, 1943, 11 p.m.

The building directly across the street from the brothel had taken a direct hit and was still smoking. Only two walls were left, both blackened skeletons, and they looked as if they were about to collapse. Occasionally a short, staccato series of pops could be heard inside the charred remains, followed by a lick of fire spurting into the night sky. *Ammo*, Ian Fleming thought. The German soldier smoked, disdainful of the real possibility of a stray shell or piece of hot debris flying at him. Fleming could not make out the soldier's insignia in the dark, but something about the man told him that confronting him would be a mistake; so he pulled out his Ballester-Molina, which he now had a superstitious fondness for, dropped to one knee, took aim and shot him, directly in the chest. Just another pop, he reasoned, among a nightful.

Fleming had arranged for the lease of the warehouse-cum-whorehouse by an Italian front company, then spent a week in Rome in late June of 1940 hiring a madam and "interviewing" prospective employees, among them Claudia Roselli. He had similarly interviewed several prospective madams before deciding on Isabella Zoppi, a former Miss Italy who had not quite finished using her beauty to get ahead. Every man, he felt at the time, should have that job at least once in a lifetime. The day after he arrived, Italy formally entered the war on the Axis side, so he did not stay as long as he might have under different circumstances.

Remaining on one knee, Fleming scanned the scene before him: the burning ammo dump, the Daimler, the dead German, the smoky night sky. No movement. He counted slowly to ten, then sprinted to the front door of the brothel, where he used his key and quietly stepped in. The large foyer was covered in a thick Persian rug. On a credenza against the far wall, a candelabra glowed, its soft light revealing the contrast between the brothel's drab, industrial exterior and its interior fittings, which tended by design toward the muted luxury so attractive to the newly, and profanely, rich. Only the best for the elite Nazi and fascist clientele he had in mind when he and Isabella set about furnishing the place and stocking its bar.

Normally there would be murmuring, laughter, and the tinkling of glasses to be heard coming from the next room, a cozy salon where the girls and their prospective clients could sip Champagne and get to know each other. But now all was deadly quiet. Fleming stopped to listen, but heard nothing. In the rear, he knew, were the girls' living quarters, including the madam's suite overlooking the river. Upstairs were the client rooms, where the rubber, so to speak, met the road. He knew where the staircase was, and was about to head for it, when he heard a thud coming from a back room, in the direction of the madam's apartment. Pistol in hand, he made his way along a dark hallway. There was a sliver of light under the madam's door. He stopped and listened.

"Get up!" a man's voice said.

Silence.

"Get up!" Followed by a soft thud.

Silence.

"Good," said the man. "You see, I have not hurt you."

Silence.

Fleming knelt and looked into the keyhole. A German officer stood with his back to the door. In front of him stood Isabella Zoppi, bleeding from a large gash on her forehead. She was in a bathrobe and her hair, which was much grayer than the last time Fleming saw her, was set in pink plastic rollers.

"One more time," said the officer.

"I do not know," Isabella replied. "Please . . ." Before she could finish her sentence, she was dead, shot in the forehead by the officer. Fleming kept his eye to the keyhole, hoping to see who else, if anyone, was in the room. The German, who Fleming could now see was an SS colonel, stepped over to Isabella, bent over, spread open her robe and looked at her naked body. This put the colonel, facing the door, at eye level with Fleming. *Beady eyes*, the Englishman said to himself. *Thin, moist lips; scar on right cheek. I think I'll kill him.*

But before he could act he heard the rapid thudding of boots on the stairway. *Bloody hell.* There was a window at the far end of the hall, with a thick blanket taped over it. He reached it quickly, tore off the blanket, raised the window and leapt out, hitting the ground hard, rolling and coming up running.

10.
Rome, July 22, 1943, 1 a.m.

"You seem to know what you're doing," said Ian Fleming.

"My boys are always falling out of trees," John Tolkien replied, "or tripping over things."

Fleming, his right leg resting on a wooden crate, a makeshift icepack on his knee, was sitting facing Tolkien in a storeroom beneath the Vatican train station. "That iodine burned like bloody hell," he said.

"It's a nasty gash," said the professor, grimacing inwardly. Try as he might, he could not get used to his colleague's casual use of coarse language. He himself had perhaps used the word *bloody* twice in his life, and those under very trying circumstances. Of course, he had to be careful about taking pride in such a simple act of omission, especially since, as he had no ear for the rhythms of profanity, it was so easy for him to forego it. "What now?" he asked. "Did anyone see your face?"

"No."

"You seem preoccupied."

Fleming nodded slightly, in acknowledgment. "I knew the madam personally," he said.

Fleming had filled Tolkien in on the night's activities, which resulted in a laceration of his knee when he slipped on the wet stone dock on his first, and last, attempt to leap into the waiting launch. His pants torn open, his knee gushing blood, Giuseppe had grabbed him by the collar and dragged him aboard.

"You were friends," said Tolkien.

"I respected her."

Tolkien remained silent. Was his young friend actually hurting in some way?

"I should have killed the German colonel," Fleming said.

"Through the door? I thought it happened in a split second."

"They always surprise me, these Nazis," Fleming replied. "But I shan't forget. I saw his face."

"What now?"

"The orphanage," said Fleming.

"What were the Germans doing there?"

"Claudia was at Via Tasso the night I found her," Fleming replied. "She must have shared her secret with Wolff, or part of it. She's too clever to reveal it all in one piece. They're looking for her."

"Speaking of secrets," said Tolkien. "The pouch came in. I've read Ultra's report."

"Ultra got involved?"

"No, they handed it off to a Cambridge classics man. It was just medieval Latin, with some Greek mixed in."

"And?"

"Archbishop Benedetti came across a stash of documents that had been lost in the confusion when Constantinople fell to the Turks in the year 1453. They traced the history of an ossuary that was in the hands of a Jewish family who had had it in their keeping for fourteen hundred years. According to these documents, when the city was about to fall, they took themselves and the ossuary to Rome."

"The bones of Christ."

"Yes."

"Is Benedetti the bishop who was blackmailing the pope? When was that, by the way?"

"Yes, he's the one. In 1735."

"So where does that leave us?"

"There's more. Among Benedetti's papers was a reference to a key, hidden somewhere in Rome."

"A key to what?

"The ossuary that holds the bones of Christ."

"Where is this ossuary?"

"He doesn't say."

"And the key?"

Tolkien shook his head. He had been pondering these very questions. "There is a notation indicating that Benedetti may have hung himself after he was excommunicated. There's no mention of the location of the ossuary or the key in his correspondence."

"Did he?" Fleming asked. "Kill himself?"

"I saw the excommunication decree," Tolkien replied, "but there's no record of a suicide, just the note. Benedetti does mention people following him. Agents of Rome, he called them."

"I'd have killed him too if I were the pope back then," replied Fleming. "What do they want you to do?"

"Bletchley Park?"

"Yes. Our masters."

"Find the key, find the ossuary, destroy the bones, if they exist."

"Why?"

"To prevent the Germans from getting them. They will use them to turn the world against the Church. Goebbels will have a field day."

"But my dear professor," said Fleming, "the Germans can throw any old bones in a box and say they're Christ's."

"Bletchley's man thinks there are documents missing. Benedetti makes reference to a list signed by St. Peter. If the Germans have these documents—if they can actually prove the bones are Christ's bones . . ."

"Their job will be much easier."

"Yes. Whether it's true or not, Bletchley doesn't want the Germans to get to the bones first."

"So how will we find this key?" Fleming asked. "And the ossuary?"

"Sister Rafaela mentioned a hidden chamber that Falco perhaps does not know exists. I'm going to ask her to take me there."

"You're being watched. I assume you know that."

"I know. The walls have eyes here. And ears."

"The Catholics have been in the spy business longer than anybody on earth," said Fleming. "I have an idea."

"Yes?"

"Become a priest. There are so many here, one more won't be noticed."

"That seems sacrilegious."

"And the idea that Christ's bones still exist doesn't?"

"I take your meaning."

"The nun is being watched, too, I'm sure," said Fleming. "Be careful. Shall I assist?"

"I'll need a priest outfit."

"Pembroke has a closet full."

"Thank you. By the way," said Tolkien, "there was a match to your photograph."

Fleming shook his head, astonished.

"He was a Jewish tailor here in Rome."

"A what?"

"He came on Bletchley Park's screen a couple of times, transporting Jews from one place to another, getting them away from the Nazis. Someone took his picture, but they left him to it."

"Did he have a name?"

"Many."

"An address?"

"He had a shop near the Piazza Navonne."

"I suppose I'll check it out."

"They surveilled him for a while. It seems he had only one client, a banker named Pietro Segreto."

"I'll check him out as well."

"Can a Jewish tailor," the professor asked, "be working for the Germans, or Falco?"

"It does seem odd, doesn't it?"

"Perhaps," said Tolkien, "there's a third party interested in Claudia's secret, someone unknown to us."

"I'm afraid there might be," Fleming replied, "but you're wrong. It would be a *fourth* party. We are officially interested as well. And by we I mean MI6, the King, the British Empire."

"Acting through us," said Tolkien. "You and me, master spies, defenders of the faith . . ."

Fleming smiled, as did Tolkien. They had been in this position before and survived, but who knew how long their luck would last? It was best sometimes to smile, and whistle past the graveyard.

11.
Rome, July 22, 1943, 6 p.m.

Pietro Segreto sat in a plush chair in his study and quietly pondered the ways of the Lord and the predicament he was in. His wife Teresa had had trouble conceiving, and when she did conceive, trouble carrying her unborn children to term. Her womb was too small. After Santino, their first son, was born, by Caesarian section, the doctors told him not to press his luck—"*non premere la fortuna, signor Segreto*"—but he did. When she was forty-five, Teresa gave birth to Luca and promptly died. And then his terrible clash with Santino, and the boy's abrupt and heart-breaking departure. Now, his health failing, his money running out, Pietro had a decision to make. He had had no choice but to give Luca—no more than a boy and a foolish boy at that—the oath, but only half of it. He had tried to give Santino, who he had not heard from in fifteen years, the same oath, but the boy had balked and run off. The boy was dead now for all he knew. And even if he were alive, what did it matter? "You are dead to me, Father," Santino had said, his eyes flat and cold, "and I am dead to you."

Pietro had been told by his father that once in nineteen hundred years had someone tried to reveal the existence of the ossuary. He had failed. At the eleventh hour, the bones had been secreted out of Constantinople and hidden in Italy. Had one of his ancestors broken the oath? His father did not know. There was nothing written, and any information that might have been contemporaneously known about this episode had been lost in the mists of time. What *was* clear was that *now*, in the Christian year 1943, and the Jewish year 5703, Europe's Jews were being systematically exterminated, like vermin, which is what the oath foretold would be the result if it was broken.

Had it been broken? Pietro found himself hoping it had, as that would make his decision less difficult. But of course he could not be sure. He only knew for certain about his current options: tell Luca the location of the bones and the key, which he felt sure would lead to their discovery, as his soon-to-be-penniless younger son was an idle fool with no skills and a voracious appetite for material things; or tell the British, in return for the lives of the fifteen thousand Jews now living in Rome. This was his dilemma. Pietro did not know, as all of his forefathers did not, what the reward for keeping the oath would be, if any. But he knew the curse that would be laid upon his bloodline and all Jews if it was broken: *They will be made a horror, an evil thing, to all the kingdoms of the earth, a disgrace, a byword, a taunt, and a curse in all the places where they shall dwell. And then they will be destroyed, to the last mother and child.*

The old banker had been generous to his friends over the years, and some of these were privy to what was said in the inner circles of the Grand Council of fascism, which he had been told was going to dethrone Mussolini in a week or two, perhaps sooner. If that happened, he had no doubt that Hitler would occupy Rome, and immediately make the eradication of its Jewish population a high priority, perhaps, given Hitler's black soul, the highest priority. Not only that, if the young whore Claudia Roselli had told Karl Wolff about the ossuary, then Hitler would order it found as his second priority. What a coup for the madman with the absurd mustache, crazed eyes, and hydrophobic mouth. He would destroy another fifteen thousand Jews *and* the Catholic Church in a matter of months. Had his ancient ancestor, Simon Beit She'an, known that nineteen hundred years later the world would go mad and Jews would be killed by the hundreds of thousands simply because they were Jews, and that the ossuary would be the means of destroying the Nazarene's church, would he have committed the firstborn sons of his bloodline, forever and without any hope of exemption, to the oath?

A hand on his shoulder shook him from his reverie.

"Sit, Carlo," he said.

Carlo Fiore did as he was told, taking a similar plush seat across from Pietro.

"What have you found?" the old man asked.

"She left the orphanage when she was twelve. Last year one of the nuns thought she saw her walking near the Campo de' Fiori."

"Is that it?"

"Yes."

"And you have your people looking?"

"Her photograph is everywhere. Cardinal Falco has seen to that."

"Isaac?"

"There are rumors about a body found on Via Statilia, near Via Tasso. It appears OVRA is investigating."

"Who knocked you on the head?"

"I still don't know." The priest still had the bandage on his head, which he fingered gently now.

"So our young whore is in hiding."

"As you or I would be. Or running."

"The whorehouse?"

"Closed."

"The whores?"

"The freight yards were heavily bombed. There is a rumor the madam is dead."

"We only have a few days," said Segreto, "a week or two at most, I'm told."

"I know."

"The whore has to be found."

"Yes. And Luca?"

"He took the oath, but I purposely did not tell him where the ossuary is."

"He knows about the bones," said Fiore. "He told the whore. She was with Karl Wolff the night I was struck. God forbid the Nazis start seriously searching. They will go to Luca first, which will lead them to you. They . . ."

"They what?"

"They torture people."

"I have been tortured all my life."

"What will you do?"

"The whore will be found. Falco has a head start. If I know Falco, he will extract Luca's name from her and then eliminate her, one way or another."

"Luca cannot keep the secret."

"Yes, I agree. I have made a decision."

"A decision?"

"I believe the oath has already been broken. I am going to give the bones to the British. I want to save as many Jews as I can before I die."

"But . . ."

"What do I have to lose? The extermination is already underway."

Fiore fell silent.

"You must leave," Pietro said. "My son will be arriving soon."

"Of course. There is something else."

"Yes?"

"The nuns at St. Michael's gave me Claudia's papers. She was born Elizabetta Tedeschi. She's a Jew."

12.
Rome, July 22, 1943, 6 p.m.

"I come up here after Vespers," said Pope Pius XII, "in the hope that a German sniper will see me from across the river and do his best to kill me. That's why I wear all white, including my zucchetto. To make an easy target."

John Tolkien had done what Cardinal Federico Falco told him to do: enter quietly, wait to be presented by the papal secretary, kneel, kiss the pope's ring, stand when bidden to, and not speak unless spoken to. *Your Holiness* was the only form of address to be used. In the hours this afternoon after he had been told that his request for a private meeting had been granted, the Englishman had experienced an inner turmoil that literally brought him to his knees, in a chapel near the train station, where he went to pray for guidance. There, the doubts about his faith that he had been experiencing were confronted by a very powerful foe: humility. In that chapel he was forced to ask himself the question he had been avoiding for months: was he a coward, afraid of the full commitment to God and His Church that true faith demanded? Now, this statement from the balding, benign-looking, middle-aged man in the round, wire-rimmed spectacles, sitting across from him on the roof garden of the papal apartments, pierced his heart, so unexpected had it been. He had been spoken to as one human being to another, yes, but he had not understood until now the full meaning of the term Vicar of Christ, for he instinctively understood what Pius meant by his seemingly macabre declaration. *You are not you, John*, he said to himself, not knowing where this sentence came from nor what it meant.

Cardinal Falco, his hands behind his back, gazing into the distance as if looking for a sniper, was standing behind His Holiness. Tolkien recalled their brief conversation a few moments ago in the large foyer of the papal apartments. "How did you arrange this?" Falco had asked.

"In the pouch," Tolkien had replied, giving himself away as a spy, but not caring. The Nazis and the fascists were his enemies, not the Church. Seeing Falco perched behind Pius, ready to take flight at the flick of the falconer's wrist, the professor wondered if this was really an accurate statement.

"My advisors tell me no rifle can reach that far," Pius continued, "but one can hope that German technology is rapidly advancing."

"Your Holiness . . ." Tolkien murmured.

"You have heard the rumors of Signor Hitler's wish to be rid of me?" Pius asked.

"Yes."

"I make myself a target because if he were to succeed, the whole world would turn against him."

The Englishman, rapt, nodded.

"People say I am not doing enough to help save the Jews, but if I were to be assassinated, this madness would end."

Cardinal Falco cleared his throat, softly but audibly.

"Enough of my ramblings," Pius said.

Tolkien nodded. This was not a question. Beyond that, the Englishman suddenly saw the great virtue in keeping silent.

"You have a very powerful friend," Pius continued, "but I would have granted your request even had it been you yourself and not Mr. Churchill who had made it."

Tolkien had not been asked to sit, but now the papal secretary, a young man in a simple, black soutane and white collar appeared from nowhere and led him to a heavily cushioned rattan chair directly opposite Pius, who nodded and said, "*Per piacere.*"

"I was terribly saddened when I was told of Father Morgan's passing," Pius said after Tolkien was seated. "And of course you must be as well. You have lost a dear friend."

"Yes, Your Holiness, I have," Tolkien replied, moving to the edge of his too-comfortable seat, his hands resting on his knees, his tongue loosened at the mention of Father Morgan. "I have come to offer my condolences. I hope I am not being presumptuous."

"Of course not, *caro professore*. I assume Father Morgan told you of our relationship."

"Yes, but . . ."

"Go on."

"I don't think he expected you to . . ."

"To what?"

"To become pope."

"Ah, yes, we were just two simple priests at the time."

Tolkien nodded, but remained silent. He knew that Pius was not a "simple priest" when he met Father Morgan in England in 1901. His family was Catholic royalty, and Pius, then Father Eugenio Pacelli, only twenty-five years old, working at the time for the Vatican Secretariat of State, was chosen by Pope Leo XIII himself to deliver condolences on behalf of the Vatican to King Edward VII after the death of Queen Victoria. He had not expected to be this awed in the presence of Pius XII, but he most definitely was. He was Roman Catholic and this was Christ's representative on earth, the man whose pronouncements on faith and morals were infallible because he spoke for Christ.

"I still confess regularly," said Pius, interrupting this train of thought. "I used to leave the Vatican and go to a local church, but I am a prisoner now."

Tolkien had formed a vague intention to bring up his suspicions about Father's Morgan's death. Indeed, that had been the foremost reason for his request that MI6 arrange the audience. But now, with the falcon eyeing him as if he were a squirrel mired in heavy snow, he saw how absurd such a foray would be. And dangerous.

"Your condolences are gratefully accepted," said Pius.

"And my services," Tolkien said. "Should you ever feel you need them."

This brought a slight smile to Pius' face. But not to Falco's. His dark eyes, hooded by thick eyebrows, locked with Tolkien's for a second and then looked again into the distance.

"They are accepted," said Pius.

"But, Your Holiness, I . . ."

"Whatever they are," the pope said. "Tell me. Do you wish anything of me?"

"No, Your Holiness. I wanted to talk about Father Morgan with . . ."

"With?"

"With someone who knew him as I did, as a friend and a priest, which you have allowed me to do."

Tolkien watched Pius as he said this. *He knows I'm not quite telling the truth*, he thought, *but does he know about this bones of Christ business? How much has Falco told him? Well, John, you have managed to lie to the face of Christ's vicar on earth. I hope you know what you're doing.*

"Perhaps, Professor Tolkien," said the pontiff, "I will call upon you for a specific service one day. I thank you for your offer."

"I am humbled that you would consider me, Your Holiness."

"Father Morgan told me about you," Pius said.

Tolkien had been told by Cardinal Falco to expect the meeting to last no more than ten minutes. He was relieved, for reasons that were inchoate at the moment, that it was coming to an end. This last statement from the pope was something he had not expected. He was sure, again for reasons unknown to him as he sat there, that it was unscripted, that is, not planned beforehand by His Holiness. He had kept his eyes cast downward for most of the visit, but now glanced quickly and briefly up at the man sitting so serenely across from him.

"He said," Pius continued, "that of all the boys at St. Philip's, you were the bravest."

"The bravest . . .?

"You risked losing the woman you loved rather than disobey him."

"My goodness . . ."

"It takes courage to obey such a command. It takes great faith in God."

"Great faith . . .Your Holiness, I . . ."

Pius stood and made the sign of the cross over John Tolkien's head, saying as he did. "*Ti benedico, figlio mio, a nome del Padre, del Figlio e dello Spirito Santo.*"

Pius must have signaled somehow to his secretary, who, when the papal blessing was complete, arrived instantly and noiselessly at the side of Tolkien's chair.

ooooo ooooo ooooo

When Tolkien and the papal secretary were gone, Cardinal Falco stood silently before Pius.

"Yes, Rico," said His Holiness.

"I have bad news."

"Yes, go ahead."

The Hawk hesitated, his lips grim.

"Speak," said Pius.

"There are three documents missing."

"What are they?"

"St. Peter's list; the oath signed by Simon of Scythopolis . . ." Falco hesitated.

"Yes, the third?" Pius asked.

"Your signed and sealed acknowledgment of the revelation concerning the bones. It was among the papers you signed when you accepted your election."

Pius looked skyward for a second, shaking his head. "Those secrets have been a burden. Fatima . . . But none heavier than this one. How could these documents be missing?"

"I don't know. Alfonso Vitale may have had a second set of keys. Sister Rafaela may have known of a secret passage."

"It is God's will. There can be no other answer."

"If they fall into the wrong hands—the Germans, the fascists—we cannot deny it's your signature and seal. They can be authenticated. The world will know we've known about the bones for five hundred years."

"It is God's will. He wants them to be found, or . . ."

"Or what?"

"I don't now."

"Your Holiness . . ."

"Leave me, Rico."

13.

Rome, July 22, 1943, 7 p.m.

"What did he say?" Claudia Roselli asked.

"He's dying."

"Dying?"

"His heart."

"Luca . . ."

"He takes digitalis all day long. His doctor says most of his heart muscle is dead."

Claudia remained silent.

"He told me," Luca said, watching Claudia's eyes, "that he would tell me where the bones are when I got married."

"Married? Was he serious?"

"I don't know. He thinks I'm a fool."

"I will marry you."

Luca could not believe his ears. He had rehearsed a conversation between him and Claudia as he made his way through the woods of his father's estate back to the boathouse. But not this conversation.

"My wife must be a Jew," he said. "I must have a Jewish heir. The oath passes to the firstborn son."

"I will convert."

They were sitting in the late-day sun on the small, wooden deck that extended from the rear of the boathouse over the lake. Below, the lake's clear water lapped gently over and around the decaying remnants of what used to be the dockage for two decent-sized boats. Claudia was wearing a light, cotton, floral-print dress, with spaghetti straps tied over her bare shoulders. She had her legs up on the deck's railing. The breeze from the lake lifted her dress' hem occasionally. It was now at mid-thigh.

"You told me I was a fool for wanting to marry you."

"No," said Claudia. "I said men say foolish things in the heat of the moment."

"Why do you want to know where the bones are, Claudia?"

"I would like to stop being a whore," she said.

"Money," Luca said.

"Yes."

"You would sell the bones?"

"Yes."

"I'm sorry I told you about them."

"You dreamt that I would marry you for love?"

"Yes, I did."

"Love is not relevant now. Will you marry me if I convert?"

"If my father tells me where the bones are, I can't tell you. I would be breaking the oath."

"You've already broken it."

"I must have been drunk. I cannot take an oath and then willingly break it. I am not entirely the fool my father thinks I am."

"You're father is dying, Luca," said Claudia. "You will be poor *and* a Jew when the Germans march in. What do you plan on doing? Opening a bank? Running? Where? They're rounding up and killing Jews all over Europe. I am your only hope."

"Why do I need you? I could sell the bones myself."

"Could you approach the Germans? You're a Jew. I have contacts in the Vatican, and with the Germans. You would be eaten alive if you approached them."

"Who, exactly?"

"Cardinal Falco, General Wolff, who will be in charge of Italy in a few days. They can bid against each other."

"They'll kill you after they get what they want."

"No. I can ruin them."

"How?"

"Believe me, I have pictures, letters, things that would destroy their careers, reduce their lives to dust."

"Even Falco?"

"Yes, even Falco."

"They were lovers, both of them." Luca could not keep the bitterness out of his voice.

"Not lovers. Clients."

Luca looked out at the lake, but saw only images of Claudia and Falco, Claudia and Wolff, in each others' arms, naked, naked and . . . "Luca!"

"Yes?"

"I am a whore. We met because you were a client. Have you forgotten?"

Luca had not forgotten. He hated himself, hated all of Claudia's clients, hated Claudia. But loved her too, madly, uncontrollably. Sexual jealousy and sexual desire were the two sides of a vice pressing against his heart.

"No," he replied. "I haven't."

"I want to stop. I want to be with you."

Luca looked at Claudia's legs, at her bare shoulders, at her beautiful, full lips. Desire was ascending. "What if he still refuses to tell me?"

"I can make him tell you."

"How?"

"First I must convert, then we must marry."

"You think conversion is a simple matter?"

"I will do whatever it takes."

"If the court does not think you are sincere, you will be rejected."

"What court?"

"The Rabbinical Court that deals with such things."

"Who is on this court?"

"Three rabbis."

"How long does it take?"

"I don't know. You will need your birth certificate and work permit."

"Why?"

"The court only deals with Italian citizens. Others have to appeal to courts in their home countries. Were you born here?"

"Yes, but I am an orphan. I have no papers. I ran away when I was twelve."

"You must have been registered at the orphanage."

"I can't go back there."

"Why?"

"I stole money when I left."

"Claudia . . ."

"There is an easier way. I have a client who can help."

"A client?"

"Yes, a client who pays me for sex. He is a master forger."

"Claudia . . ."

"Yes?"

Silence.

"When we get married, when we're rich," Claudia said, "I will stop being a whore."

"Get rich by selling the bones of Christ."

"I doubt they're the bones of Christ, but yes, I would."

Luca remained silent. Claudia's dress was now at her panty line.

"We can be rich, Luca," said Claudia, "and do what we want." After she said this, she lifted her dress to her waist and pulled off her cotton panties, one leg at a time. "Kiss me, Luca," she said.

Luca leaned in and put his arm around her, but Claudia took his head in her hands and guided it downward. "Not on my lips," she said. "Here. It's time you learned how to pleasure a woman. It's time you became a man."

14.
Rome, July 22, 1943, 11 p.m.

The cassock that J. J. Pembroke had provided John Tolkien had thirty-three buttons in front from collar to hem, "for the thirty-three years Christ was on earth," the station chief had said. The professor fingered them now as he knelt in a pew in a private, unnamed chapel located along a seldom-used hallway near the Vatican Library on the ground floor of the Apostolic Palace. He had set the bolt-lock when he entered and fumbled in the dark to light the two small candles on either end of the altar rail. "Christ will be looking at you," Sister Rafaela had said, and she was right. The candles shed very little light, but enough so that he could make out the crucifix hanging from a thick chain behind a worn marble altar. The candlelight reflecting in Jesus' deep-brown eyes made it seem as if he was looking directly at the Englishman. *Of course*, Tolkien said to himself.

Known informally as the sanctuary chapel, because it locked from the inside, the windowless room was small, dark and sparse, with two short rows of shaky pews. The looming crucifix, with its starkly realistic Christ figure, slumping and in pain, who seemed always to be looking at you, was its centerpiece, the magnet that drew tortured souls to the room. On the altar's face was etched a passage from John: "If ye believe not that I am he, ye shall die in your sins." *Perhaps I should come to mass here on Sunday*, Tolkien said to himself. *I may not feel like such a hypocrite.*

He had been in the chapel for fifteen minutes or so and was beginning to wonder. Fingering the buttons, he decided that when he reached the last one he would leave. As he felt for the thirty-third button, Sister Rafaela appeared behind the crucifix and beckoned to him.

When he reached her, he saw that there was a trap door at the rear of the altar, its shape barely discernible in the dark, and that the fragile old nun was bidding him to descend first, which he did.

"You gave me a fright," said the professor when they reached the bottom of a ten-foot ladder and he was standing on a damp, stone floor. "Where are you?"

"Here," she whispered. She had lit a candle as he was asking his question. "Come," she said. Her features blurred by the golden candlelight, her dark eyes deep-set and luminous, she looked more like a ghost, or a biblical angel, than a ninety-year-old nun.

The professor followed her along a meandering and intensely dark stone corridor. "Are we in a cave?" he whispered.

"Catacombs."

"How did you find them?"

"There are catacombs under my dormitory as well. I have lived there for seventy years. When I became old and useless, I was often left to my own devices. I started to explore. One of the passageways leads to the sanctuary chapel, and to here."

"Did you tell Father Morgan about this?"

"Yes, we planned on coming here but he died the night before."

At the end of the corridor they came to a room with an ancient wooden door that was swinging askew on one hinge. They entered and Sister Rafaela raised her candle. Its soft light revealed four walls lined with stone lintels, like mantelpieces, all empty. Scattered on the floor were dozens of bones, small hips and ankles, delicate wrists, intact skulls, shattered skulls, tiny knee caps, all lying among the remains of perhaps twenty stone boxes, all of which had been smashed into many pieces.

"Ossuaries," said Tolkien.

"Yes, children's ossuaries. We won't need my tool." The nun had brought a small pickaxe with her, which she had removed from the front pocket of her tunic when they entered the room.

"Is this how you found them?"

"No, Cardinal Falco has been here."

"What did Father Morgan say exactly?" Tolkien asked.

"That the key was buried with martyred children."

"Are these martyred children?"

"I believe so. There are no markings. The early Christians did not mark their graves for fear of desecration."

"Are there other children's catacombs?"

"I don't know of any."

"*With* martyred children? Is that what he said?" Tolkien had gently taken the candle from Sister's hand and was stooping to take a closer look at the broken ossuaries.

Sister Rafaela did not answer.

"Sister," Tolkien said.

"Cardinal Falco killed Father Morgan," she said.

"It does seem so," said Tolkien. "Sister."

"Yes?"

"What exactly did Father Morgan say about the key?"

"That a martyred child was sleeping on it."

"Let me have your tool," said Tolkien

Several of the ossuaries were partially intact. He bent over one and tapped on its floor. It was solid stone. As was the next. The third was hollow. It broke easily, revealing a leather pouch the size of a fist. Tolkien stood and untied the pouch's leather lacing. He reached in and pulled out a gold ring with a silver box that looked much like a tiny ossuary set on it. On the box's top façade was a crucifix set in precious stones.

15.
Rome, July 23, 1943, 10 a.m.

"We cannot find the whore," said Guido Leto.

"So I've been told," Karl Wolff replied. "I am disappointed." Of course, Leto knew that Wolff was more than disappointed. The soon-to-be Nazi-in-charge-of-all-of-Italy would not have ventured to Leto's office at the Stablimento de Mattazione slaughterhouse in Rome's bleak Testaccio neighborhood if he were merely disappointed. Why this particular whore was so important, Wolff had not deigned to tell him, and Leto had learned it was best not to ask too many questions of his German masters. They were unpredictable, to say the least, both in the manner and the substance of their responses.

"We will keep looking," Leto replied.

"Does she have a family?"

"She was an orphan."

"The orphanage? Have you checked there?"

"Yes. Nothing. She is barely remembered. But someone else was there asking."

"Who?"

"A priest named Carlo Fiore. He works for Cardinal Falco."

Wolff looked over to Otto Skorzeny, who was sitting on a couch off to the side. Wolff and Leto were facing each other in comfortable leather chairs.

149

"Do you know why Falco is looking for the same whore we're looking for?" Wolff asked.

"No."

"She must have teased him with the same information she teased me with."

"Yes," said Leto, "I agree."

"Your great Il Duce is in trouble, but I suppose you know that."

"I do."

"I will do my best to assist him."

"As will I."

"We will not let the Allies walk into Rome," Wolff said. "When we take over, we will put an apparatus in place, but for now I am relying on you."

Leto nodded and swallowed quietly. There was no mistaking the threat Wolff was conveying. He could feel Skorzeny, with his ugly scar and slitted eyes, looking at him, but thought it wise not to turn his way.

"You know," the German general continued, "you will be hung by the Allies if they win the war?"

"Yes, I do."

"The whore has information that will prevent that."

Leto nodded. After fifteen years as the head of Mussolini's secret police, with unfettered power to imprison, exile, or kill anyone he deemed anti-fascist, Leto himself had become the cornered rat. "I do have something you might be interested in," he said.

"What?"

"The night that you last saw the whore, a body was found on Via Statilia, two blocks from this building."

"*Ja*, and?"

"It took us a while to identify it. It was a Jew we had been looking at."

"Go on."

"We think he was getting Jews out of Rome."

"Legally?"

"And illegally."

"Both are very expensive."

"Yes."

"Who killed him?"

"We don't know."

"What time was he killed?"

"Virtually the same time the whore left Via Tasso."

"You think there's a connection?"

"Possibly. It is a strange coincidence."

"Where did he get the money, your dead man, to pay for all these heroic acts?"

"A banker named Segreto, another Jew."

"*A banker. A Jew.* Why are your Jews so free to maneuver here? Is someone protecting them? Your precious Church?"

"No. We have laws similar to your Nuremburg Laws."

"But you don't really enforce them."

"We do. Jews can't hold public office or government jobs. They can't teach school. They . . ."

"In Germany," interrupted Wolff, "we have taken all their money and property. All of it. And put them to work in camps. The same in Poland and Hungary, Austria, Czechoslovakia. There are no Jewish bankers in these countries helping other Jews. There are no Jewish bankers in these countries, period."

Leto remained silent. Thus far Mussolini, the only person he answered to, had not terrorized Italy's Jews with quite the same passion as Hitler terrorized Germany's. That would change when the Germans took over Rome.

Wolff turned to Skorzeny. "Arrest this banker," he said. "I have a feeling he knows something about these so-called bones of Christ."

"Yes, Herr General," Skorzeny replied. "It will be done."

"And you," Wolff said to Leto, "keep looking for Claudia."

"Claudia?"

"The person you refer to as the whore."

"Oh, yes, *certo.*"

"You are presumptuous, Guido."

"Presumptuous?"

"Suppose for a moment that I was in love with her?"

"With . . .?"

"The whore."

Silence. Leto, balding and unprepossessing, like many sadists, forced himself to look straight ahead, to affect a slightly puzzled look on his pasty face. Wolff was expressionless, unreadable, and Skorzeny, he knew, without having to look, was smiling broadly.

"Not to worry," said Wolff, smiling. "I'm not. But . . ."

"But . . ." said Leto.

"I do want her found. If she is not found soon, *I* will have you hung."

"Yes, my general, *certo, natürlich,* of course. I . . ."

"I am teasing you, Guido," said Wolff. "You are much too valuable to hang. Do you agree, Otto?"

"I agree."

"So," said Wolff. "How goes it with our other nemesis, your communist friends? The ones killing your agents like they are wounded pheasants? Or perhaps I should say fish in a barrel, a more apt metaphor."

"I have two in hand right now," said the Italian. "Would you like to meet them?"

"Meet them?"

"A local lawyer and his priest, both members of the Prelature."

"The Prelature?"

"Opus Dei. They do God's work."

"Ah, I've heard of these madmen," said Wolff. "I'd be delighted. But, Guido, surely Opus Dei cannot be godless communists."

"The lawyer is," Leto replied. "We followed him to confession, where he would have to be truthful in order to be absolved of his sins."

"Hence the priest," said Wolff, smiling.

"Yes," said Leto. "Follow me."

Leto, much relieved to have changed the subject of his hanging, however much in jest it may have arisen, led the two German officers out of his office and down a long corridor, at the end of which two Italian soldiers stood guard in front of a steel door.

"Open," said Leto.

One of the soldiers unlocked the door and swung it open. Leto gestured and smiled and the three men entered a freezing-cold meat locker, rectangular in shape. Large, stainless-steel hooks hung from a steel track on each side of the ceiling. These were all empty except for two, from which hung two men by the backs of their necks, a priest and a man in a dark suit. Ice had formed on their hair and faces and exposed hands.

"A priest and his penitent attorney," said Leto. He gave both bodies a slight shove, setting them to swaying gently on their hooks

"Did they talk?" Wolff asked.

"The lawyer didn't," Leto replied, "but the priest did, violating one of his sacred oaths."

"Excellent. He is now in Catholic hell," said Wolff. "And?"

"We are rounding up a cell as we speak," said Leto. "They will all hang." He was lying. The attorney had taken cyanide and the priest had refused to say anything except to politely suggest that his interrogators return to hell, from whence he was sure they had come. But Wolff would never know. He would soon be too occupied with stopping the advancing Allies to worry too much about the assassinations of Mussolini's secret police.

16.
Rome, July 23, 1943, 11 a.m.

"I have some interesting news," said James Pembroke.

John Tolkien and Ian Fleming, sitting across from Pembroke in his cramped office, remained silent.

"The banker," said Pembroke, "who your tailor worked for, Signor Segreto?"

Silence.

"He's asked for a meeting."

"So he knows we've identified him," said Tolkien.

"We must have a mole," said Fleming.

"No to both," said Pembroke.

"Then what?" Fleming asked.

"He's the one who sent his rabbi to me, the one who knows Claudia Roselli's secret."

"Then he could be the one who tried to have her killed," said Fleming. Pembroke, Fleming, and Tolkien had discussed the issue of the identity of the person or organization that wanted Claudia dead. Neither of the obvious candidates made sense. Karl Wolff could have had her killed while she was at Via Tasso three nights ago. And Fiore, Falco's man, had made no attempt to follow Claudia when she exited Via Tasso 145 that night. "The tailor worked for Segreto," Fleming continued. "He could have been following her and waited in the alley for her to walk by."

"How did he know?" Tolkien asked.

"Know what?"

"That Claudia knew this dark secret."

"He probably had a mole in either the Vatican or Via Tasso," said Pembroke. "More likely the Vatican. No one's who they seem here. And every Italian I know is either scheming to get out or to get rich before the country is ground to dust."

"I think," said Tolkien, "that she revealed only part of her secret to Falco and Wolff. They wanted the rest, the meat, so to speak. She was probably playing them against each other. Segreto, or whoever tried to kill her, wanted to prevent her from telling them."

"So," said Fleming, "he must know the whole secret."

"And now he wants to sell it to us for the lives of fifteen thousand Jews," said Tolkien.

"We can't deliver that," said Pembroke. "The Nazis will be here in force in a few days."

"What *can* we deliver?" Tolkien asked.

"Money," said Pembroke. "Which he can use to continue his work."

"What about logistical support?" Tolkien asked. "Commissions, passports, passage on ships?"

"We'll try, but no promises," the station chief answered. "Once Hitler takes over Rome, most of our efforts will be to support the resistance and our troops in Italy."

"When and where?" Fleming asked.

"Five today," said Pembroke, "at his villa on the Appian Way."

17.
On The Appian Way, July 23, 1943, 5 p.m.

"Did you find out anything about the ring?" Ian Fleming asked.

"Yes," John Tolkien replied, "Sister Rafaela knew immediately what it was."

"What is it?"

"It's a Jewish betrothal ring."

"With a crucifix in gemstones on it?"

"Which of course sets this one apart."

"I should say so."

With Fleming driving a battered Lancia borrowed from the Americans' fast-growing collection of assets, he and John Tolkien were bumping along the Appian Way south of Rome. A hot sun—the temperature was nearing ninety degrees Fahrenheit—was beating down on them through a cloudless, pale-blue sky. Fleming, in shirtsleeves and linen trousers, was resting his left arm on the car's open window ledge, smoking a Morland Special in its tortoise-shell holder. With his head jauntily tilted and the usual mischievous gleam in his eye, he looked to Tolkien more like the American president than a dilettante spy. The professor was dressed as a priest who might be working quietly in his rectory: black shirt, pants, socks, shoes, white clerical collar.

"These rings," said Tolkien, "were common at the time of Christ. They were used as keys to open dowries, mostly symbolic. They were engagement rings, if you will. Sister Rafaela has seen pictures in the archives."

"Jewish engagement rings in the Vatican archives?"

"You'd be amazed what the archives hold," said Tolkien. "There are two letters from Abraham Lincoln to Pius IX. Mary Queen of Scots wrote to Pope Sixtus V while awaiting execution. The decree excommunicating Martin Luther is filed chronologically."

"Goodness."

"There are over forty miles of shelving."

"How do you know all this?"

"Father Morgan and I corresponded, and Sister is a trove of knowledge."

"And this ring, or key," said Fleming, "you think it's to the ossuary that holds the bones of Christ?"

"I believe it's the key that Benedetti talked about, the one he mentioned as being buried with children. It must have been hidden by someone when the so-called ossuary came to Italy in 1453. Benedetti must have come across references to it."

"*So-called?*"

"I doubt it exists."

"Whether these bones exist or not, I must say, one has to admire Benedetti's nerve," said Fleming. "To blackmail the pope, to threaten to destroy Christianity."

"I've told you several times," said Tolkien, "if the bones exist, it doesn't mean that Christianity is falsely premised. Christ rose bodily into heaven. There were eleven witnesses."

"He just happened to leave his bones behind."

Tolkien shook his head slightly and considered making a comment about the moral vacuity of cynicism, but refrained. He wished sometimes he could actually call himself cynical, rather than the traitor that in his darkest moments he felt himself to be to a faith that had been rock-solid since child-hood. One could be jolted out of cynicism, but *treason?*

"You think me a cynic," said Fleming. "I'm just an accurate observer. If there are bones, there must be doubt. You surely can acknowledge that."

"The Nazis will surely take that tack if they should find the bones," Tolkien answered. *Yes, John, avoid the issue of doubt.*

"You're still writing I take it," said Fleming, concentrating on the raised and skewed surface of the ancient road. "This would be a story to tell."

"Yes."

"Frodo and the gang?"

"Yes."

"What are they up to?"

"Frodo and his best friend are trying to save the world."

"Like you and me."

Tolkien smiled.

"Do they have help?"

"A wizard, an elf, a dwarf."

"Where do you get these crazy ideas?"

"I've been writing about wizards and elves and dwarfs for twenty years."

"Yes, but why?"

"At first it was to entertain my children."

"And now?"

"To get to know myself; to find out what I believe."

John Tolkien had never asked himself the question posed by his young colleague. *Why else, indeed,* he asked himself now, *would a person write fiction?* And then he asked himself another question, out of the blue: *Why else indeed would a person adhere to a certain faith?* Or *was* it out of the blue? He would not have been comfortable in any theatrical costume, but his priest garb was particularly unnerving in light of the doubts he had been having about his faith over the last few months. He blamed the war, all the unnecessary death and suffering, but he knew that was facile, cowardly actually. Perhaps it was God himself who had decided recently to put black cloth on his back and now Fleming's seemingly innocent question in his mouth.

"I say," said Fleming. "That would never have occurred to me."

"I suppose you could put it to the test," said the professor.

"By writing, you mean?"

"Yes."

"I may not like what I see."

"It will be the real you, though. That's worth a lot."

"I repeat."

"You can change, you know."

"You mean it's never too late to become a decent sort of fellow? Unselfish and all that?"

"Yes. You'd need an agent, of course." *That was a leap,* Tolkien said to himself. *Save yourself first.*

"You mean to peddle my books?" Fleming asked.

"No, to change," Tolkien replied. "I don't see you doing it on your own."

"Goodness, we *are* hammering old Ian Lancaster today."

"Sorry," said the professor. "This priest suit is making me self-righteous." *Change the subject, old man,* Tolkien said to himself. *Old Ian doesn't want to look into the abyss. And neither do you.*

"Not to worry," said Fleming, flicking cigarette ash out of his open window, "my skin is thick and my memory thin."

"You *do* remember," said Tolkien, "what Pembroke said about the checkpoint on this road?"

"I do."

"I think that may be it up ahead."

"Is your collar straight?"

"Yes." Tolkien did not have to look in the rearview mirror. He had been meticulous in donning and double-checking his priest's garb before setting out. An Irish priest traveling with an Irish ex-pat arms dealer to visit a sick relative. What could be better cover in desultory, fast-sinking, Italy?

"Just nod and smile."

"I'm good at that."

"All that training."

"Yes."

"You remember who we are?"

"Mr. Bond and Father Le Chiffre."

"Good solid names, don't you think?"

"I think Le Chiffre will confuse them. I'm supposed to be Irish."

"Exactly."

"Where did you get Bond. It's prosaic. It shouts fake."

"My insurance man in London."

"Really?"

"Yes. It's real, so it can't be fake."

"One can only hope."

"Remember, if they ask you a question, answer in gibberish. I'll say it's Gaelic."

"I'll speak in Elvish."

"Even better. No chance these dagos know that tongue."

18.

On The Appian Way, July 23, 1943, 5 p.m.

John Tolkien sat in the Lancia under the pounding sun and watched as Ian Fleming, for the moment arms dealer James Bond, completed his interaction with the Italian *colonnello* at the checkpoint. Pembroke had said that the Italians were defeated and looking frantically for cover, but the professor had expected at least a semblance of military diligence. The colonel had actually put his arm around Fleming when he introduced himself. Now Fleming was stepping back and saying something that Tolkien caught snatches of. *Si, caro colonnello, a Londra a mano . . . Attendere . . . prego, caro colonnello . . . uno momento . . .* and walking toward the Lancia.

"We're fine," said Fleming when he reached the passenger window. "Can you reach into the glove box and hand me the cigarettes." Tolkien did as he was asked, handing Mr. Bond the four packs of Morlands. "Leave two behind," said Fleming, "I'm running low."

"It seemed easy," said Tolkien, replacing two of the packs and handing Fleming the other two.

"It was. He asked me if I could help get him to Ireland after the war. Perhaps get him a position with my company. He's an armaments expert, you see."

"Goodness, and me?"

"He barely looked at your papers. Very respectful of the clergy. He let another priest pass a few minutes ago."

"A full colonel?"

"He says the rank and file are deserting in droves."

"I say," said Tolkien, nodding slightly, looking over Fleming's shoulder. "We have company."

Behind Fleming, on the inbound side of the checkpoint, a long, black, dust-covered Daimler had stopped and its occupants emerged. One, a German SS colonel with a thick scar on his left cheek, was approaching his Italian counterpart. Fleming assessed this scene in the Lancia's side mirror, tilting his head casually to get a full view. Behind the Daimler was a small, open-bed truck with perhaps ten Waffen SS troopers sitting on its sideboards, machine guns slung across their shoulders. Fleming straightened and turned to look at the two colonels, who were only twenty meters away, standing on the other side of the checkpoint's makeshift barrier arm, a long pole that hooked onto a small hut at one end and that swung on wheels at the other.

When the two colonels looked his way, Fleming, smiling broadly, waved to them and pointed to the two packs of Morlands in his hand. "I'll head over," he muttered to Tolkien. But before he could take a step, Tolkien swung open the passenger door, thumping Fleming out of the way, emerged from the Lancia and fell to the ground clutching at his collar.

"What in bloody hell . . .?" said Fleming as he knelt next to his colleague.

"Heat stroke," said Tolkien. "A sick priest is better cover than a healthy priest."

"I . . ."

But Fleming could say no more. The two colonels had approached and were looking down on Tolkien. Fleming looked up and immediately recognized Scarface as the officer who had shot Isabella Zoppi pointblank in the forehead in San Lorenzo two nights ago.

"*Was ist das?*" said Scarface.

"Heat stroke," said Fleming, working his fingers under Tolkien's white clerical collar and ripping it open. "*Hitzschlag.*"

"Heat stroke?" said the German colonel. "Who are these people?"

The Italian colonel, whom Fleming had thought both a buffoon and venal—quite a combination—now stood erect and said, in perfect clipped German, "An Irish priest, high in the Church, on his way to visit a dying relative. His papers are in order."

Tolkien had opened his eyes and was attempting to rise, but Fleming pushed him back.

"Stay," he said, in German. "I'll get water." Then to the Italian colonel: "May I?"

"You may not," said Scarface. "Who are you?"

"He is . . ." said the Italian.

"I am not speaking to you," the German barked. He was staring down at Fleming, who was staring up at him, their faces only a foot or two apart. Fleming's Balester-Molina was in a compartment beneath the floor of the Lancia's glove box. His right hand itched for it.

"May I stand?" Fleming asked.

The German nodded, and Fleming got to his feet.

"I am James Bond," said Fleming in his excellent, albeit English-accented German, "an armaments representative. Irish."

"You sound English."

"I was in school in England for many years."

"Where?"

"Eton."

"Your neutrality sickens me."

"There are those in my country who would side with Germany," said Fleming.

"Don't assume we would have you," said Scarface.

"Of course, Herr Oberst."

"How were you injured?" the German asked. He was staring at the bandage above Fleming's eye.

"I'd rather not say," said Fleming, glancing down at the supine Tolkien, who was doing an excellent job of looking overheated and ill.

"You'd rather not say?" said Scarface. He was glowering.

"In a whorehouse," Fleming whispered. "I was . . ."

"Yes, you *were* . . .?"

Fleming again glanced down at Tolkien, whose head was now lolling to one side. *Was he hiding a smile, the blackguard?*

"I . . ."

"I don't want to hear about your perversions," said the German. "You disgust me." He then turned to his Italian counterpart. "You looked at their papers?"

"Yes, *certo.*"

"Did you search the car?"

"No, I . . ."

"Have your men do it now."

The Italian barked an order and two of his men rushed over and began going through the Lancia. As they were doing this, the *colonnello* barked another order and another of his men brought over a canteen, which the Italian took and, kneeling, placed against Tolkien's lips. Before rising he poured some of the water into his hands and rubbed in on the professor's face. "*Non siamo animali qui,*" he said under his breath. "We are not animals here."

It took only a few minutes for the two Italian soldiers to go through the Lancia. When they were done, one of them, a corporal, stood erect facing his superior. "*Niente,*" he said, "*Mio colonnello.*"

The Italian colonel dismissed the soldiers, who headed back to the hut.

Tolkien had lifted himself to a sitting position and now reached his hand to Fleming, who grasped it and hoisted him to his feet.

"*Er maara, hanta,*" Tolkien said to the Italian colonel.

"*Cosa?*" said the colonel.

"It's Gaelic," said Fleming. "He says *grazie.*"

"Ah . . ."

"Enough," said Scarface. "I am in a hurry." And then to Fleming. "Herr Bond, do you have an inventory list with you?"

"No, I'm sorry. This is a personal excursion."

"What does your company deal in?"

"We make parts for your Mauser HC, your Walther P38, trigger guards, barrel plating. The Italian army buys parts from us for their Astra 300 and 400. We have a contract with Steyr-Daimler to make the Maschinengewehr 42, the same as your troops are carrying." Fleming nodded in the direction of the open bed truck.

The German colonel fingered his scar and stared at Fleming, his eyes flat but piercing. None of what Fleming said was true, but he had been taught that whenever a cover was adopted as much homework as possible was to be done. He had spent an hour talking German weaponry with Pembroke before heading out. Did Colonel Scarface-Woman-Murderer believe him? Now would be the time to attack, but all he had were his hands and feet which meant he could land a swift kick to the Germans balls, but that he and Tolkien would certainly be killed. Fleming began counting in his mind. When he got to four, Scarface interrupted his thoughts. "Deal with them as you wish," the German said to the Italian, then turned abruptly and headed back to his staff car.

19.

The Villa Segreto, July 23, 1943, 5:15 p.m.

"Is he dead?" Claudia Roselli asked.

"Yes," said Carlo Fiore.

Luca Segreto, who was kneeling over the body of a man lying face up on the floor in front of his father's desk, rose slowly to his feet. In his right hand was a blood-smeared envelope. "Yes, he's dead," he said to Fiore. "Who are you?"

"What was that?" Fiore asked. Luca had slipped the envelope into the front pocket of his pants.

"It's addressed to me, from my father," Luca replied. "Again I ask, who are you?"

"I am Father Carlo Fiore, a friend of your father." Fiore was in his street clothes—black shoes, black pants, black shirt, and white clerical collar. His shiny black hair was swept back, fully exposing the small facial craters left behind by the smallpox that had destroyed his looks as a boy and set him on the path to the priesthood. The hair above his right ear had been shaved and a white bandage taped on his scalp.

They all looked down at the body—Luca and Claudia on one flank, Carlo Fiore on the other—at the clean entry wound over the heart and the plume of blood spreading on the Persian carpet beneath it.

"Who is he?" Claudia asked

"Old Silvano," said Luca.

169

The French doors behind Pietro's desk were open to the late afternoon sun and heat. Claudia and Luca had entered through them a few moments earlier to find Fiore standing over Silvano, his rosary beads in his hand.

"Have you seen your father?" Fiore asked.

"I spoke with him last night," Luca replied, "but not today. Who *are* you?"

"I told you, a friend of your father."

"A priest who kisses a Jew's ring?" said Luca.

"How do you know that?" Fiore asked.

"I saw you."

"My ancestors were *conversos*," said Fiore, "Jews who converted to Catholicism during the Inquisition to escape persecution."

"So you are a Jew *and* a Catholic priest."

"Yes."

"Which comes first?"

"The human being comes first."

"You are Cardinal Falco's man," said Claudia. "The one who's been following me." Claudia's mind was on the blood-stained envelope in Luca's pocket. She had broken her silence only in hopes of diverting Fiore's attention away from it. *Do not give it to him, Luca.*

Fiore nodded. "And you, Claudia," he said. "What are you doing here?"

"Luca and I are getting married." *That should divert him.*

"The old man has no money," said Fiore. "Even the estate is mortgaged."

"I love Luca."

"I'm sure you do."

"Why were you following me?" Claudia asked. "Was that your man who tried to kill me on Via Statilia? Is Rico a murderer now?"

"The cardinal would like to speak to you."

"How did you hurt your head?" Claudia asked. Ian Fleming had told her of the priest he had knocked out just before rescuing her.

"You are too clever for your own good, Claudia," Fiore replied.

"Who tried to kill me?"

"I believe it was Pietro."

"What?"

"I told him what you told the cardinal about the bones of Christ."

"My father?" said Luca. "It can't be. You are a devil to say such a thing, a monster."

"Your father has a secret," said Fiore, "that has driven him to the brink of madness."

"You mean the bones of Christ?" said Luca.

"Yes," Fiore replied, "which you foolishly revealed to Claudia and which she revealed to his eminence, and God knows who else. I pray not General Wolff, one of her prized clients."

Luca's eyes narrowed and lips tightened at this. He opened his mouth to speak, but before he could form whatever he was about to say, his eyes darted to something behind Fiore.

"What are you looking at?" Fiore asked.

"Is one of you Pietro Segreto?" said Ian Fleming, who, along with John Tolkien, was standing a few feet behind the priest. He had a gun in his right hand, pointed at Luca.

"Ian!" said Claudia.

Fleming nodded. "You look like you've seen a ghost, Claudia," he said. "I thought we were friends."

"You know this man?" Luca asked Claudia, who nodded and murmured, "Yes I do."

"Well?" Fleming said. "Pietro Segreto? Is he here?"

"No," Luca said, "my father is not here. Who are *you*?"

"We work for the British government," Fleming answered. "Your father asked us to meet him here at five."

"I looked through the house when I saw Silvano," said Fiore. "Pietro is not here."

"And who might you be?" Fleming asked.

"I am Father Carlo Fiore, assistant to Cardinal Federico Falco."

"Is Silvano the dead fellow?" Fleming asked, nodding toward the corpse.

"Yes, Silvano Pascucci," said Luca, "my father's man."

"Who shot him?"

"We don't know," said Fiore. "Pietro asked me to meet him here at five as well. I arrived to find the house empty and Silvano dead."

"Does Pietro have a head of white hair?" said John Tolkien. "Thick white eyebrows?"

"Yes," said Luca, staring intently at Tolkien. "Why . . .?"

"We passed a German staff car on the way here," said the professor. "There was such a man in the back seat."

"You don't say," said Fleming.

"I saw him at the checkpoint," said Tolkien, "while you were palavering with *il colonnello*."

"Ah, so that's why old Scarface was in such a hurry," said Fleming.

"Are you saying the Germans have my father?" said Luca.

"I'm afraid so," said Fleming. "It looks like old Silvano here tried to protect your father and was killed for his efforts."

"The Germans . . ." said Luca.

"Yes," Fleming replied, "the Germans."

"Where will they take him?" Luca asked.

"OVRA headquarters on Via Tasso, I would imagine," Fleming replied. "Or perhaps . . ."

"Perhaps what?" Luca asked.

"The old slaughterhouse where they hold some prisoners."

"Will they let us see him?" Luca said.

"Claudia," said Fleming, ignoring Luca, "what are you doing here?"

"We're getting married," said Luca.

"I see," said Fleming, and then to Claudia: "Does your betrothed know he's living in the twentieth century? Does he think OVRA has visiting hours at their prisons? Does he even know what OVRA *is?*"

The room grew quiet as all eyes turned to nineteen-year-old Luca Segreto. "I will kill you," he said to Fleming. His fists were clenched at his side, his face flushed. Claudia took his hand and moved closer to him.

"No you won't," said John Tolkien. "You are worried about your father. We will contact the authorities. We will do our best to free him. We are here to help."

"You must have a son," said Claudia, who was stroking Luca's arm, to Tolkien.

"I do, three of them."

"Why did my father want to see you?" Luca asked, looking first at Fleming and then at Fiore. Though there was still anger in his eyes, Claudia's nearness seemed to have calmed him.

"I suspect he wanted to strike a bargain about the bones with these two gentlemen," said Fiore, indicating Tolkien and Fleming. "And then enlist my help."

"A bargain?" said Luca.

"He and I have been getting Jews out of Italy for the past five years," Fiore replied. "The Nazis will be taking over soon. I believe he was going to tell Mr. Fleming and Mr. Tolkien where the bones are hidden, in return for the help of the British government in getting Rome's Jews safely away."

"The bones of Christ?" said Tolkien.

Fiore nodded. "Yes."

"Do they . . .?"

"I don't know," the priest replied.

"How would Pietro Segreto know about them?" the professor asked.

"His family," Father Fiore answered, "has been keeping their location secret for two thousand years."

"He confided all this to you?" said Tolkien.

"Yes. I sought him out when I learned of my Jewish blood. I considered converting, but he discouraged me. 'The Germans are killing Jews,' he said. 'Stay where you are. You can help me.' He asked me to help him get Jews out of Italy, and I agreed."

Tolkien stared hard at Fiore.

"I am a Catholic," Fiore said, "if that's what you're thinking. But I did not hesitate to help Jews in distress, as I am also a Jew, and a human being, and the Church has done little."

"Unfortunately," said Fleming, "it is the Germans Pietro will soon be telling the location of the bones."

"What will the Germans do with the bones?" Luca asked.

"They will hang them over Pius' head," said Fleming, "and make him their puppet."

"The Church will not want the world to know that Christ left his bones behind," said Tolkien. "How to explain that to the masses after two thousand years? In case my colleague wasn't clear enough, the pope will be made to side with Germany in the war."

"My father will not tell them where the bones are," Luca said to Fiore, his voice rising, hatred in his eyes, "*and he is not a murderer.*"

Claudia gripped Luca's arm tighter. She was beginning to feel sorry for him, for the first time to understand his pain. Fiore had mentioned Karl Wolff as one of her prized clients. Then Ian Fleming, whom she had slept with just three days ago, had suddenly appeared and she had felt the color leave her face. Had Luca seen that? No one, aged nineteen or ninety, likes to be confronted with his lover's former lovers. *God*, she said to herself, in one of her rare entreaties to the supreme being, *please, no more surprises today.*

PART III

THE SAVIOR

1.
The Vatican, July 23, 1943, 5:15 p.m.

"How was Turkey, Rico?"

"Painful."

"I am sorry to have sent you in such a mad rush."

"It had to be done."

"I want to know what you've learned," said Pius, "but first tell me of Mussolini."

Pope Pius XII and Cardinal Federico Falco were seated across from each other in Pius' rooftop sanctuary. The setting sun had slipped behind a bank of wispy clouds, diffusing the light that reached them to a soft pink. The bombing of Rome in mid-July had lasted only three days, but the two prelates were no different from the rest of the city's inhabitants in wondering if they would hear the roar of Flying Fortresses at twilight approaching from the north.

"There is no hard intelligence," Falco replied. "My guess is that Badoglio's people are moving him around."

"He has friends, I suppose," said Pius.

"Loyal fascists, yes," said Falco. "And then there are the Germans. They will want to rescue him. It doesn't look good that Hitler's puppet has been kidnapped."

"General Wolff wants to see me."

"Yes."

"I will put him off a few more days."

"I understand, but you will have to see him. Rome is completely in Hitler's hands and he can make it difficult for you."

"Not to mention kill me."

Falco gazed over the parapet in the direction of the setting sun. "There will be no weapons allowed when you meet Wolff," he said.

"Of course."

"And don't drink or eat anything."

"I won't. Now tell me about Turkey."

"In Istanbul," said the cardinal, "I could find nothing. The Ottomans left the churches standing, but destroyed all the archived documents. Archbishop Roncali did a complete investigation, at my request, prior to my arrival. Nothing exists, no records prior to 1453."

"Benedetti?"

"At the time he wrote to Clement, in 1735, he was living in quarters near St. Anthony of Padua. The building still stands. It is now a small convent. We found nothing there."

"There is more, I assume," said Pius XII, "or you would not have asked so urgently for this meeting."

"I went to Selcuk," Cardinal Falco replied, "where Benedetti was born. The pastor of the local church there, Father Basil, took me to a room under the church where parish baptismal and marriage records are kept. I found Benedetti's baptismal certificate. Under it was this." Falco handed Pius a sheaf of yellowed papers bound with a purple and gold ribbon. The one on top had the seal of the Apostolic Vicariate of Istanbul on it.

"What do they say?" said Pius. He did not take the papers from Falco's hand.

"When the Ottomans were at the gates of Constantinople, the reigning bishop, one Louis Pellatiere, tried to preserve what he thought was important in the Cathedral—crucifixes, chalices, candlesticks, correspondence, other documents. His people hid as much as they could in a cellar beneath an outbuilding. Chaos ensued when the Muslims broke through. Pellatiere was killed. Two hundred years later, when that building was razed during Benedetti's reign, workers uncovered Pellatiere's trove. These letters were among the documents."

"What do they say?"

"In 1453, the Ottomans were besieging Constantinople. The city was defended by massive chains strung across the entrance to the Golden Horn. A Jewish banker in Constantinople, Shimon Yehuda, offers Pelletiere a large amount of gold to allow one of his ships to slip past the chains. Pellatiere refuses, thinking it is a trap. Yehuda offers more money, but Pellatiere still refuses. Finally Yehuda tells Pellatiere that his family has been keeping the bones of Christ since the Crucifixion. They are kept in an ossuary made by his ancestor, Simon of Scythopolis, at the time of Christ's death and resurrection. There is a special key that opens the ossuary. They also have St. Peter's list of the objects to be buried with Christ and the original oath, on parchment, signed by Simon of Scythopolis, and his son, Joseph. Yehuda is concerned that the Ottomans are going to massacre Constantinople's Jews and that the ossuary and parchments will be destroyed or lost. Pelletiere is skeptical, but agrees—he apparently needs the money—on the condition that his men crew the ship and accompany Yehuda and the ossuary to their final destination. The last letter is a report from Pelletiere's captain. He tells Pelletiere of the remarkably swift and trouble-free voyage to Rome, of his sailors kneeling in vigils around the clock before the ossuary, though its contents were unknown to them. He himself, the captain, at Yehuda's request, arranged to hide the key in the catacombs beneath St. Peter's. His brother was a priest assigned to the Holy See. He was entrusted with St. Peter's list and the original oaths on parchment. Presumably he gave them to the reigning pope, Nicholas V. These we still have, as you know, or did until recently."

Pius waited a moment to make sure that Falco was finished, then said, "So it is true."

"It seems so."

"And Benedetti used these letters to try to blackmail Clement XII."

"Yes."

"And was excommunicated for his efforts."

"Yes."

"Did Clement have him killed?"

"Father Basil took me to the ruins of Ephesus, to an aqueduct. He pointed to an iron ring attached under an arch. Benedetti, he said, reached down, tied one end of the rope to the ring, the other around his neck and jumped off."

"Father Basil knew of this as a fact?"

"It is local legend accepted as truth."

"And the bones?"

"Nicholas ordered them buried. The captain mentions taking them north, to the Apennines, but he doesn't say where."

"How do you know this?"

"It was in the captain's last letter."

"The key?"

"The Englishman, Tolkien, has it."

"How do you know this?"

For the first time since the meeting began, Falco hesitated.

"I want to know," said Pius, "if I have a sin to confess."

"One of my agents is Sister Rafaela's confessor," said the cardinal. "She and Tolkien found the key in the catacombs."

"I would like to meet Sister Rafaela."

"You can't. She received communion the morning after her confession and died later that day."

"Having been absolved."

"Yes."

"She is in paradise."

"Yes."

"With Father Morgan."

In the silence that followed this remark, Pius' gaze remained steadily on his chief of intelligence, the man charged with keeping him alive, and keeping the Church intact, during the firestorm that was World War II. The cardinal looked away, finally. Had he killed Father Morgan?

"No," the Hawk said, "I didn't."

"You wouldn't tell me if you did," said Pius, nodding slightly to acknowledge to Falco that he had indeed answered his unspoken question. His Holiness was not smiling, but there was no anger in his eyes or edge to his voice. He was sick at heart though, as he now believed it likely that Falco had indeed killed the kindly old English priest. Falco's sins were his sins.

Forgive us, Lord. Forgive us.

2.

The Villa Segreto, July 23, 1943, 5:15 p.m.

"Believe it," said a voice. "He would have killed me too, if he could have found me."

Luca and Claudia turned in the direction of the voice and saw a tall, handsome, dark-haired man of thirty or so, in the rugged clothes of a day laborer—dusty work boots, rough denim pants, a cheap cotton shirt, a sweat-stained red bandana around his neck—standing in silhouette between the open French doors. At his waist, bulging beneath his shirt, was the outline of a handgun.

"Who are *you*?" Luca asked.

"I am Santino Segreto, your brother," said the man in the doorway, who now stepped into the room, where he could be clearly seen. The three of them stood still for a long moment, taking each other in—Luca and Claudia on one side, Santino on the other—across the dead body on the floor between them.

"It can't be," said Luca

"It is," said Santino.

The brothers stared at each other as if each was looking in a mirror. The structure of their proud faces, their lustrous dark hair, their piercing hazel eyes, were exactly the same.

"Who are *you*?" Santino said to Claudia, who was looking at him in disbelief. *Figaro.*

183

"I am Claudia Roselli," she replied, holding her breath, unable to remember if she had told the man who had taken her virginity, and changed the course of her life, her full name.

Santino looked from Claudia to Luca and back to Claudia, a wry smile on his face, a smile denoting *what*, Claudia could not tell exactly, though she did not think it denoted recognition. It looked more like salaciousness to her. Salaciousness as in, *You have grown up, younger brother.*

"Who killed old Silvano?" Santino asked.

"The Germans," Carlo Fiore replied.

"And who might you be?" Santino said, staring at Carlo Fiore.

"Is this really your brother?" Fiore asked Luca.

"Yes," Luca replied.

"Are you sure? You haven't seen him in—in how many years?"

"I'm sure."

Claudia looked at Luca, whose face was white, and thought, *Yes, he's sure. Is this your last surprise for the day, Lord?*

"Where is Pietro?" Santino asked. "I have come to finish what we started thirteen years ago."

"He's a prisoner of the Germans," said Ian Fleming.

"And you?" said Santino, looking at Tolkien and Fleming. "Who are you?"

"Did your father tell you about the bones of Christ?" Fleming asked.

"Who *are* you?" Santino repeated.

"He's going to tell the Germans," said Fleming. "We'd like to prevent that. We're British agents."

"*You* have to stop them?" said Santino.

"I suggest you stay out of it," said Fleming. "You'll get killed."

"I have been fighting the fascists in Greece and Italy for the past ten years," said Santino. "I am not afraid of them."

"Fighting the fascists?" said Fleming.

"Yes."

"On your own?"

"I am a communist."

"I thought all the communists in this part of the world, young and old, were dead or in exile," said Fleming.

"I lead my own group," said Santino. "We kill OVRA agents."

"What do you know about the bones?" Fleming asked.

Santino smiled wryly and shook his head. "Shall I trust them, little brother?" he said to Luca.

Before Luca could answer, Tolkien spoke up. "The Germans will be here in force soon," he said. "They will round up Rome's Jews. Your father was trying to prevent that. We hoped to be able to help him."

"You *hoped*," said Santino.

"Shall we lie to you?" Tolkien asked.

"Yes," Luca blurted. "I trust them. It's them or nothing, them or Hitler."

"Of course, little brother, I agree," said Santino. "These devils are better than the German devils, or the pope's devils. My father," he continued, facing the Englishmen, "tried to make me take an oath. He told me about the bones of Christ, about an ossuary hidden in Little Tibet. He was about to tell me where, but I stopped him. I wanted no part of his oath. To me it was a sign of madness—he had been going slowly mad since my mother died giving birth to Luca. I turned and left his study. He told me as I was leaving that if I revealed any of what he had said he would have me killed. He had a second son, he said, he would give the oath to, the terrible secret."

"Is that why you ran away?" Luca asked.

"Yes."

"Why did you return? Did you want to take the oath?"

"Yes, but to then sell the bones. I need money for arms, explosives, supplies. We are isolated in the mountains. I want to do more than assassinate OVRA agents. They are cowards and easy prey."

"You were going to deceive our father."

"Yes."

Claudia, her eyes hooded, watched as the brothers—one hard, the other soft, one strong, the other weak, one a heartless man, the other a wounded child—stared at each other.

"Little Tibet?" asked Tolkien, breaking into these thoughts.

"The Apennines," Santino replied. "He was always looking at maps of the Gran Sasso area. He had one on his desk when he tried to give me the oath."

"That's a rather large mountain range," said Fleming. "Does Little Tibet refer to the whole range, or just a portion of it?"

"The whole range," said Santino.

"So," said Fleming, "we're in the dark; but if your father revealed the location to the Germans, they're probably heading north as we speak."

"He wouldn't," said Carlo Fiore.

"They'll torture him," said Fleming.

"He told me he'd kill himself if the Germans took him."

"How?"

"His foxglove. He kept a special box with him at all times. Enough to stop his heart instantly."

"I have comrades in those mountains," said Santino. "They will let me know if the Germans start looking around, or show up at a certain place."

"We'll help," said Fleming.

"No," said Claudia, who had dragged Luca over to Santino, so that the three of them were now standing together facing Tolkien, Fleming and Father Fiore. "The British will do the same thing," Claudia continued, "blackmail the Church, if they get the bones."

"We will do no such thing," said Tolkien. "We simply want to prevent Hitler from getting the bones."

"Is it money you want, Claudia?" Fleming said. "Let us help and we will pay handsomely."

What do *I want?* Claudia asked herself. Luca had taken her hand, a simple but suddenly unnerving act. Before she could answer, the phone on Pietro's desk rang. Frozen in place, they all stared at it as it rang a second time, as if it might have been Christ himself calling to clear up the question of the bones.

"Pick it up, Luca," said Tolkien. "This is your house."

Luca did as he was told, said *pronto* into the receiver, and then *si, Luca.* After listening for a moment, he said *grazie,* and hung up.

"My father's body," Luca said to the group, "was just dumped on the steps of his bank. That was his manager. He is having the body brought here."

3.
The Papal Apartments, July 25, 1943, noon

"The brothers and the woman," said Cardinal Rico Falco, "are staying in the boathouse at the villa. Father Fiore saw the younger brother take something, a letter he believes, from the old servant's pocket."

"They will be sounding the Angelus soon," said Pope Pius XII.

"Yes, Your Holiness."

"You are impatient."

The two men were sitting in the large parlor of Pius' living quarters in the Vatican. Behind them were the French doors, open to the sultry day, of the small balcony from which Pius, and many popes before him, said the Angelus prayer and homily on Sundays. The murmuring of the crowd in St. Peter's Square below could be heard drifting up through the open doors.

"Do you know when the Angelus began?" Pius asked.

Falco shook his head. "No."

"No one does, really," said Pius. "Perhaps in the twelfth century. Farmers worked until dusk then. As the sun began to set, the local church would sound its bells. The farmers said three Hail Marys before leaving their field."

The Hawk remained mute.

"The crowds have been much larger lately," said the pope, nodding toward the balcony. "Our flock is less and less afraid of Signor Mussolini and his band of killers."

"I agree," Falco replied.

"What do you think was in this letter?" Pius asked.

"A map, perhaps. We don't know."

"If it was a map, why are the Segreto brothers still here?"

"A good question. They must be waiting for word from someone. The older brother is a fanatical communist, a member of a cell that specializes in killing OVRA agents. He cannot travel openly. Perhaps they are waiting for forged papers, perhaps help from other cell members. If they leave, we will follow."

"How will you know when they leave?"

"We have made a deal with the woman."

"The prostitute."

"Yes."

"What kind of deal?"

"We will provide her with diplomatic papers, a flight to Geneva and . . ."

"And what?"

"A large sum of money, very large, double whatever the British offer her."

"How hard it is to be truly moral," said Pius.

"Yes."

"You don't want the British to find the bones."

"No, they will put their national interests ahead of the Church's."

"I disagree."

"Your Holiness?"

"Professor Tolkien," said Pius, "found the key for a reason."

"Your Holiness?"

"You are repeating yourself."

"I am . . . I . . ."

"I don't want you or Fiore or your men touching the ossuary. I want Tolkien to be the one."

"The Englishman? He writes of pagan things."

"He is more devout than you or me."

"He may destroy it."

"Yes. Or not. He will decide."

"But how . . ."

"You will assist him in any way you can. Tell Father Fiore those are my instructions."

"Your Holiness, this Tolkien may use it against us."

The tolling of the bells ringing out the Angelus could now be heard.

"He may do anything he wishes," said Pius, who rose and turned to look toward his balcony, to listen to the Angelus being tolled and the crowd beginning to call, *Papa, Papa.* Turning back to the Hawk, he said firmly, "Now leave, and never speak to me again of this matter."

4.
Calascio, Italy, August 1, 1943, 9 a.m.

"I repeat: He said 'Rocca Calascio,' and then he dropped dead."

"We have been through the castle several times, Otto," said Karl Wolff. "Did he say anything else? Anything more specific?"

"No."

"You tried your best?"

"Yes," Otto Skorzeny replied, "we told him we were holding his son, that we would kill him if he didn't cooperate. We also had his pants down and a knife to his balls."

"In the car, this was?"

"Yes, as soon as we passed the checkpoint."

"And that's when he said 'Rocca Calascio'?"

"Yes."

"And then immediately died?"

"Yes."

"And you think that good information?"

"Yes."

Skorzeny had done his job. After killing the old man who had absurdly tried to prevent him from capturing the old Jew, he had caught Segreto fumbling with a silver pillbox in an inside pocket of his suit. This he took away and then hustled Segreto into the waiting staff car. The knife to the balls had worked wonders before and there was no reason to believe that it had not worked with the banker. No one wanted to bleed out after his testicles were cut off. It was no way to die. The fact that the Jew *did* die was a coincidence. He seemed about to say something else, but there was no need to tell Wolff that. What good would that do?

"My people tell me he was ill," said Guido Leto. "His heart."

"Perhaps you should have let me know," said Otto Skorzeny.

The three men were sitting in heavy rattan chairs on a wide, sundrenched patio at the rear of a small villa in the hills above Calascio, an Apennine village that was much the same in 1943 as it was in 1443, except for the small garrison of Waffen SS troops that had set itself up on a level plain just outside the town's once fortified but now crumbling protective stone wall. Above the town stood the gray, depressing ruins of Calascio Castle—Rocca Calascio—a thousand-year-old rock fortress abandoned in the fifteenth century after an earthquake destroyed half of it. On a glass-topped table between the three men was a metal tube, embossed with a swastika, and a leather folder, similarly embossed, tied with a red cord.

"What would you have done?" Leto replied. "Brought along a physician?"

Otto Skorzeny had risen to pour himself a cup of coffee from the carafe on the service trolley that a female member of the commandeered villa's staff had rolled out for them. A quite beautiful, Aryan-looking female member of the villa's staff, who had stood primly by the trolley, her head slightly bowed, her hands clasped on her starched white apron, before being dismissed with a nod from Wolff. Why the general would keep the staff, an old couple and their young niece, Wolff did not know and did not inquire. Generals, especially this one, Hitler's hand-picked head of all Italy, were kings, with whys and wherefores unto themselves. He, Otto Skorzeny, was a soldier, and nothing else. Silhouetted against the morning sun, Otto turned, coffee cup in hand, keeping his eyes flat and expressionless, and looked at Leto. He then looked across at Wolff, who shook his head, almost imperceptibly, but unmistakably. "We need him," Wolff had said before Leto arrived, "to keep the locals in line. Do not antagonize him."

"I should be joining my men," said the scarfaced colonel, ignoring Leto, but not his condescension.

"Let me show you this," said Wolff, who reached for the metal tube. He unscrewed one end and pulled out a large sheaf of coiled vellum paper. This he unscrolled and spread out on the table, placing heavy ashtrays at either end to hold it open. Skorzeny moved closer and looked down at a large, color rendering of a columned palace of some kind. At the bottom right were the initials AS and the date July 25, 1943. Below the date was another set of initials.

"This is Speer's rendering of the Führermuseum," said Wolff. "Himmler sent it to me by special plane yesterday. The Führer wants it to house the bones of Christ. It is to be built in Linz, Hitler's hometown. The bones will be proof that the resurrection was a sham, that Hitler is the true savior, Nazism the true religion. Those are the Führer's initials below Speer's."

"The Church will claim they are not Christ's bones," said Skorzeny, who had barely glanced at the rendering. "How can we prove such a thing? The Führer might be put in an embarrassing position." Otto had been sent personally to Italy by Hitler to find and rescue Mussolini. His abduction was an insult to the Reich, an insult that had to be avenged. But Herr General Wolff, Himmler's friend—and who knew what else— had involved him in this absurd search for Christ's bones. The delay chafed so much he decided to risk challenging Wolff, something that very few subordinates alive, if any, would do. But this digging under a decrepit castle was not soldiering, and he wanted above all else to be soldiering.

"Not when we show the world what's in this," said Wolff. He picked up the leather folder, opened it and spread its contents, two obviously very old documents, and one new one, on the table. The three men stared at them.

"What are they?" Skorzeny asked.

"This," said Wolff, pointing, "is the list of the things to be buried with Christ, drawn and signed by St. Peter and Joseph of Arimathea. This," Wolff continued, moving his finger, "is the oath signed by the first of the keepers of Christ's bones. And this is an affidavit signed by Pius XII in 1939, acknowledging that he had seen the first two documents."

"And this means?" Skorzeny asked.

"When a pope accepts his office," said Wolff, "the Church's deepest secrets are revealed to him. The prophesies of Mary to the children of Fatima, for example. That the bones of Christ are preserved somewhere is obviously one of those secrets. If we find the bones, these papers will prove they are truly Christ's. We will expose as false the major myth of Christianity. The high priests at the Vatican will be made to look like just another group of charlatans getting rich off gullible peasants. We will have eliminated a major enemy of the Reich."

"How did you get these?" said Leto. "That is clearly the signature of Pius XII, and his seal."

"It doesn't matter," Wolff replied. "They are real, believe me."

Skorzeny knew when he had lost. Whether these pieces of paper meant anything or not, Wolff believed they did, and so did Leto, a home-grown papist if there ever was one. Defeated, he nodded to Wolff.

"Do not fret, Otto," said Wolff. "Guido has people everywhere. Mussolini will no doubt be located. Until then, stay here, help me find these bones. They may be guarded. It may take a fight. There are communist cells in these hill towns who have surely noted our presence. They may need dealing with."

Skorzeny nodded curtly. "Of course."

"Good," said Wolff. "Thank you. The bones, by the way, may be under the castle, not in it. Guido says there is a local legend about something supernatural hidden in the mountain beneath the castle. Apparently there are catacombs and a network of caves. He is going to ask the mayor for assistance. There must be locals who know the secrets of the mountain. It will not be difficult to get their cooperation."

"That may be more difficult than you think," said Leto. "The locals think that the world will end if the mountain beneath the castle is disturbed. That what is hidden should remain hidden."

"I see," said Skorzeny. "The whole world." Despite Wolff's admonitions, he could not avoid a tinge of sarcasm in his voice.

"Some say it's a dragon," said Leto.

The two German officers looked at Leto.

"These are peasants," said the Italian. "These dark stories are in their blood. Believe me, they fear the monster in the mountain more than they do the Wehrmacht."

"Not after we're through with them," said Wolff. "I want to know every cave, every tunnel that leads under the castle. Round up the town's children and put them someplace until we get answers."

Leto nodded.

"Now tell me, Guido," said Wolff, "what happened at Villa Savoia? You were there."

"Victor Emmanuel dismissed Mussolini as prime minister. Mussolini had been criticizing the Grand Council in high fashion, his face red as a beet. The king cut him off in mid-sentence. He told him he was appointing Badoglio prime minister, and renouncing the Ethiopian and Albanian thrones. Mussolini turned white, but before he could speak he was arrested."

"And you, the head of OVRA, of Italy's Gestapo, weren't told where he was taken?"

"No."

"I suppose Victor Emmanuel and Badoglio don't trust you."

"They know I am loyal to Il Duce. I am head of his state police. I was invited only because of the confidential information I have on everyone of importance in the Italian government. They fear me."

"What did they do with Mussolini?"

"He was put into an ambulance and was gone in a matter of minutes."

"What is Badoglio up to?" Wolff asked.

"He has stated publicly that he will continue the war on the side of the Axis, but he is secretly negotiating with Eisenhower."

"Personally?"

"No, he has sent three generals to Lisbon to meet with General Bedell, Eisenhower's man."

"Will he surrender?"

"He wants Rome protected, but yes, he will."

"When?"

"Soon. One month, two months."

"What will happen when Italy surrenders?" Wolff asked.

"There will be civil war," Leto answered. "Some will join the Allies, some will remain loyal to Mussolini."

"Hitler will consider it a betrayal of course."

"Of course."

"He will disarm and intern the Italian army."

Leto nodded.

"We will take control of the Balkans, the Dodecanese, et cetera."

Again Leto nodded.

Otto Skorzeny was listening intently to this conversation. He did not care about Italy's role in the war from this point on. The Italians had never been of any real assistance, never true allies. Nor had he been keen on kidnapping the pope, a mission now put on hold until Mussolini was rescued and returned to power. He knew without having to hear it said that to do such a thing as kidnap a sitting pope would turn the tide of the war against the Fatherland. His job was to find Mussolini, whom the Führer himself had described as a dear friend. This job, unfortunately, would have to wait until this business with the bones was finished.

"What will *you* do?" Wolff asked Leto.

"I will join Il Duce."

"And remain loyal to us."

"Yes, of course."

"If we find him."

"Yes."

"If we don't find him, you will be a war criminal. The Americans will hang you, unless the communists cut your balls off first."

"Yes."

"So, Guido," said Wolff, "tell me, where is Il Duce? You must know something."

"Badoglio's people are moving him from place to place. Where he is at the moment, I don't know, but I will find out soon enough."

"Not too soon," said Wolff, winking broadly. "I want Otto to help us find the bones of Christ. For *that*, our names will go down in history."

"Unless we blow the whole world up doing it," said Skorzeny, this time more than a tinge of sarcasm in his voice. "History will then come to an end, of course."

"By the way, Guido," said Wolff, smiling, "if the citizens of this backwater do not help us find the ossuary, it will be you who will kill their children, one per day, until they do."

Leto nodded.

"Do you understand?"

"Yes."

"I don't doubt your loyalty."

"I . . ."

"But I believe in removing temptation."

5.

The Villa Segreto, August 3, 1943, 2 p.m.

Claudia Roselli, nude, hoisted herself onto the boat-house dock, grabbed a towel from a cleat on a dock post and began drying off. When she was finished, she wrapped the towel around herself, drew a cigarette from a pack on a nearby blanket and lit it with a beautiful gold lighter she had taken from the villa. Exhaling, she took a moment to assess the Segreto brothers, who, in swim trunks, were sitting in frayed canvas chairs on the edge of the lake some fifty meters away. She had, of course, already noted the similarities in their strikingly handsome faces, the faces of medieval Roman nobility mixed with Middle Eastern wildness. Half Michelangelo, half Saladin. And the obvious differences, such as Santino's confident body language versus Luca's attempts to hide his youthful awkwardness, his feigned sophistication.

Looking at the brothers Segreto, their beautiful bodies bathed in golden sunlight, she found herself, for the first time ever, intrigued by the inner man. What was in their hearts? What were they made of? A week ago, she would have been shocked that she would ask herself such questions, the questions of an amateur, but Claudia was nothing if not honest with herself. Her world had changed, and she was about to set off on a journey whose end she could not fathom. Aware that they were watching her, she threw her cigarette into the lake, turned, and slowly walked the length of the dock to the men.

"You are discussing the letter," she said, when she reached them. Gazing from brother to brother, careless of the slipping towel, tilting her head, she used both hands to squeeze lake water from her long, dark-brown hair. Some of it dripped onto a leather satchel on the grass next to Luca, the satchel that Claudia knew at one time contained the letter that Luca had taken from old Silvano's jacket pocket, a letter from Pietro with a crude map describing the exact location of the bones of Christ in a stone chamber deep under the ancient Apennine fortress, Rocca Calascio. And also describing, in a separate drawing, a key hidden in a catacomb under the Vatican.

"Yes," said Luca.

"Where is it?" said Santino.

"I told you," Luca replied. "I burned it."

"Where are the bones?"

"If I tell you, will you help me hide them again?"

Claudia, lifting the towel up so that it again fully covered her breasts, looked from brother to brother. *Orphans now*, she thought, *who are no comfort to each other. No, more than that— who distrust each other. Why else would Luca tell his brother he had burned the map?*

"I am the first son," Santino replied. "Father wanted to tell me where they were."

"But you ran away, instead," said Luca.

"I . . ."

"He wants the bones," said Luca. "For his communist friends."

"And why do *you* want them?" Santino asked.

"I don't," Luca answered. "I want to keep the oath."

"Do you have a son to pass it on to?"

"No, but one day I will."

"Yes," said Santino, looking up at Claudia. "If your betrothed still wants you. She wants the bones for herself, or have you forgotten?"

"You say that word with such contempt," said Claudia, surprised to find herself so staunchly defending the concept of betrothal.

Santino, looking intently at her and then casting his gaze aside, did not respond. *Does he know who I am?* Claudia asked herself. *Can he be jealous?*

"The years have made him bitter," said Luca. "He does not believe that two people can love each other. He believes only in the Communist Party. He loves only the downtrodden workers of the world."

"Our father made me bitter," said Santino, "poverty made me bitter, the war made me bitter . . ."

"Have you heard from your colleague?" Claudia asked.

"Yes," said Santino, "a messenger arrived a few minutes ago. You were out swimming."

"What did he say?"

"We were right to wait. The Germans are swarming over Rocca Calascio. They are looking for a secret way into the mountain, under the castle. They have killed two children to show how serious they are. The townspeople are trying to help them, desperately trying."

"Your father must have said something," said Claudia. "But he obviously did not tell them the way in."

"No."

"We have to go," said Luca. "They are killing children. They will stumble upon the bones.

"Yes," said Claudia. "We can argue about the bones when we find them."

"We will first have to get the key," said Luca.

"There is no time," said Claudia. "The Germans are breathing on the bones. We will find a way in."

"Guido Leto is there," said Santino abruptly, "and Karl Wolff."

Claudia stared at the older Segreto brother. In his dark eyes was the most utter determination Claudia had ever seen. No wonder he saved himself in the sea that day, with nothing to cling to but his will to live.

"I will kill them both," said Santino.

"How many Germans?" Claudia asked.

"Two hundred," Luca replied. "More arriving every day."

"Will you kill them all?" Claudia asked Santino.

"Yes."

"You've lost your mind," said Luca.

"I have colleagues in the hills," said Santino. "They will gladly help."

"We should leave tonight," said Claudia. "I'm going up to bathe."

"To the villa?" Luca asked.

"Yes. I like running water and inside plumbing."

"You'll miss them on the road," said Santino. "We won't be staying in luxury hotels."

"What true communist would?" Claudia replied, before turning to leave.

∞∞∞∞ ∞∞∞∞ ∞∞∞∞

In the villa, Claudia threw the towel on Luca's bed and brought the telephone over to the tall window overlooking the terrace. She liked the idea of talking to a cardinal while naked in front of a window. Maybe the Hawk was flying above and could actually see her with those fierce, glowing eyes of his. She used to tease him sometimes, standing at the foot of the bed, slowly undressing. She would tease him again now. If only she had a way to reach Karl Wolff. She would tease *him* as well. She was the only person who knew exactly where to find the most amazing discovery of all time, the bones of Christ. Except for Luca, but he didn't count. His stupidity astonished her. Keep the oath? No one was that idiotic, or that naive.

6.

Calascio, August 4, 1943, 7 a.m.

"Is that the church?" said Ian Fleming.

"Yes," Carlo Fiore replied.

"What are all those people doing?" said John Tolkien.

The three men were lying on their bellies behind a low rock outcrop high in the Apennines, from which they had a direct view across an open, arid plain to the octagonally shaped, three-hundred-year-old Church of Santa Maria della Pieta. The small square in front of the church was filled with people, all peasants, some standing, some kneeling and praying. On either side of the church's wide front door stood SS troopers with machine guns unslung and aimed at the crowd. Rocca Calascio stood on a mountain top behind the church. The shadows of the castle's ragged towers fell across the people in the church courtyard. Fleming had brought binoculars, but there was no need to use them. The church was only fifty meters away, the castle two hundred, with nothing in front of either or in between them but rocky, open plain. To the left they could see the rooftops of the village of Calascio, and a few last villagers making their way up the steep, dirt road to the churchyard. Through the crystal-clear mountain air the three men could easily see the terrified looks on the faces of the townspeople and the scowls on the faces of the soldiers.

"I . . ." said Fiore, but before he could finish his sentence, the church's oaken front door swung open and two more troops emerged, dragging a young boy between them. The crowd moaned in unison, like a chorus in a Greek tragedy. A woman in the rear took a step forward, howled and then charged at the soldiers. She was shot by the two door guards, falling dead in her tracks. The other soldiers then threw the boy to the ground and shot him dead. The crowd fell instantly silent, the looks on their faces no different than had they seen the devil himself appear and eat the child. A man in jodhpurs, high boots, and an absurdly decorated military tunic emerged from the church and said something to the crowd, emphasizing his words with lashes of a riding crop.

"Guido Leto," said Carlo Fiore.

"What are you doing?" Fleming said to Tolkien. Looking down Tolkien saw that he had his colleague's forearm in a death grip. John Tolkien did not answer. He released his grip. Then he fingered the ossuary ring he had attached to a cheap chain and placed around his neck. Was it vibrating? No, it couldn't be. It was his heart beating, beating so hard that it must be causing the ring to . . . to what? *To moan*, the professor thought. *Dear God, it's moaning.*

7.
Calascio, August 4, 1943, 8 a.m.

"They'll kill another child tomorrow," said the tall, blond woman known only as Maria to her comrades.

Santino Segreto did not wonder at Maria's matter-of-fact tone of voice. They had both had first-hand experience of the Germans killing women and children. Your heart turned to stone. You killed them back, as many as you could. You hoped you died before the war ended so that you would not have to remember. "Do the townspeople know about this cave?" he asked.

"They must," the woman replied. "The same families have been here since time began. It leads nowhere, so whatever it is the Germans are looking for they won't find here."

"What are they looking for?" Santino asked.

"A secret passage under the castle. It must be treasure."

"Where is the rest of our group?"

"There is another network of caves on the other side of the Gran Sasso Hotel."

"Can they help us?"

"There is Italian army activity in the area. We don't know why."

"Are they searching, scouting?"

"Yes, and they have set up a perimeter around the hotel. My comrades are stuck there. They cannot cross to us. We are on our own."

"Where are my brother and the woman?"

"Sleeping in another cave."

Santino had been sleeping when Maria found him. He and Luca and Claudia had taken an old farm truck from a barn on the Segreto estate and driven it through the night on back roads to the outskirts of the town of L'Aquila, where they rendezvoused with a boy of no more than ten, who led them along mountain trails until they reached the cliff top that overhung the cave they were now sitting in. Santino rose and walked toward the front of the cave where, staying in shadows, he peered out at the stark, treeless landscape that was the high Apennines. Little Tibet, the Italians called it, and he could see why.

"We can't be seen from here?" he said.

"No," Maria replied. She had joined him at the cave's entrance. "From below, the face of the mountain looks like sheer rock. You'd have to know precisely where to descend to find it."

"And then you'd probably fall to your death," said Santino, remembering the short, but treacherous descent of the night before."

"You stepped on my head," said Maria.

"Sorry. Those footholds . . ." They had belayed down to the cave, the thin rope around his waist not much comfort to Santino.

"Why are you here?" Maria asked.

"To kill Germans."

"I warned you away. There are too many."

"There are never too many."

"I don't believe you."

"You think I came here for you?"

"I have no time for love now."

"Neither do I."

They looked at each other for a beat or two, Santino remembering the night they met ten years ago, when he was twenty-two, she twenty. His second virgin. He had no luck with them.

"Tell me, Santino," said Maria, "what are the Germans looking for under the mountain? The townspeople talk of monsters, of untold treasure."

"I don't know."

"I think you do."

The older Segreto brother shook his head. "Thank you for helping me."

"I told you not to come."

"But you sent the boy."

"Did I have a choice?"

"You could have said no."

"The innkeeper was frantic. He is a cousin. Everyone is related in these mountains. You are a wanted man."

"Who is the boy?" Santino asked. "He led us here in pitch black."

"My nephew, Pietro. 'Capretta,' he is called."

"He is new to me."

"His parents were sheep farmers, living mostly in the hills. They were killed two weeks ago by the Germans, accused of helping the partisans. Capretta found his way to me."

"*The little goat*," said Santino. "He knows these mountains?"

"Every cave, every hollow, every path, every peak."

"How many Germans in the camp?"

"Two hundred."

"Who is the commandant?"

"Karl Wolff."

"Wolff?"

"Yes."

"Officers?"

"A colonel named Skorzeny. Leto is here as well."

"I don't believe it."

"Leto has put on his fascist clown uniform and is overseeing the children at Santa Maria."

"The church?"

"Yes, he's living there. They shoot the children in the courtyard."

"How many children?"

"There were thirty-three, now there are thirty. I was able to send a warning. Many others went to nearby towns or are hiding in the mountains."

"Guards?"

"Eight German soldiers."

"Is Wolff living in the camp?"

"No, at a villa on the hillside. I am a servant there."

"How did you manage that?"

"The owners departed when the war began. They left their servants behind—my aunt and uncle. I was living with them when Wolff appeared. I am a maid. I serve lunch. I scrub floors. I watch and listen. I am due back in an hour."

"Can you get me in?"

"Yes."

"Can Capretta carry messages?"

"Yes."

Santino was silent, gazing at the miles of high, rolling mountain plain before him, and the peak of Gran Sasso, the highest in the Apennines, in the distance. He had come to Calascio to find the bones of Christ, to sell them to the highest bidder, but that would have to wait. It was probably a fool's errand anyway.

"You never told me you had a brother," said Maria, breaking into Santino's thoughts. "Is he one of us?"

"He's a child."

"Then why is he here?"

"We're Jews, do you forget?"

"And the woman?"

"A whore, my brother's fiancée."

"A whore and a fiancée in one person?'

"Yes."

"There's something you're not telling me."

"Will you help me kill Wolff and the colonel, and Leto?"

"Yes."

"It will have to be soon. Today. No more children must die."

Maria nodded.

"There is another thing you can do for me."

"Yes?"

"It is for the cause."

"What?"

"My brother has a map that he thinks will lead him to a secret cave under the castle. Get it."

"So there *is* treasure."

"I doubt it, but if there is, we'll use it to fight the fascists."

"How shall I get the map from him?"

"You are a woman."

"And what will happen to your brother?"

"His whore will abandon him."

"A good thing, you believe."

"Yes."

"Does he love her?"

"He thinks he does."

"I will try, but . . ."

The thud of a rock hitting the bottom of the canyon some fifty meters below the cave stopped Maria in mid-sentence. Santino looked at her quizzically, and she put her index finger to her lips. Then another thud.

"Maria," a voice from above said.

"Come," she said.

A moment or two later, two people swung over the brow of the cave onto the ledge that fronted it. Luca and Capretta. They stepped into the cave.

"Where is the woman?" said Maria.

"Gone," said Luca.

"Gone?" said Santino.

"She must have left in the night."

"We should have guarded her," said the boy.

"We have to go," said Maria. "She can lead them right to these caves. *Now.*"

8.
Calascio, August 4,1943, 10 a.m.

"Halt," the SS corporal said, his voice sharp and clear in the hot morning air.

"A woman," said his fellow trooper, a private. Both were expert marksmen, both, from behind chest-high sand bags, had their machine guns trained on Claudia Roselli, who had stopped, her hands in the air, when ordered to, some fifty meters from the guards.

"*Sprechen Sie Deutsch?*" the corporal asked.

"*Ja,*" Claudia replied.

"*Bewaffnet?*"

"*Nein.*"

"*Entkleiden.*"

Claudia did as she was told, dropping her clothes, except for her brassiere and panties, to the ground next to her.

"*Alle,*" said the corporal.

Claudia complied, placing one hand at her breasts and the other at her thickly covered mons veneris when she was finished.

"*Vortreten,*" said the corporal. He was smiling, as any man would who was lucky enough to see Claudia in all her statuesque glory, her legs long and shapely, her waist tiny, her breasts full and pendulous, her ass high and round and plump.

9.
Calascio, August 4, 1943, 2 p.m.

The three men—Carlo Fiore, a real priest; John Tolkien, a fake priest; and Ian Fleming, a fake arms dealer—sat under a merciless Italian sun, their backs to the low stone outcrop that overlooked the fortress-like church of Santa Maria della Pieta. Fiore and Tolkien had removed their clerical collars and rolled up the sleeves of their black shirts, feeble attempts to cool off. Fleming had taken his shirt off and wrapped it around his neck to soak up the sweat. On the ground between them were the remains of a lunch of bread, cheese and figs, along with three Italian sub-machine guns and three Italian hand grenades. Occasionally, over the past hour, since Fiore had returned from D'Aquila with the food and the weapons, one of them would turn onto his stomach to peek over the rocks. This Ian Fleming had just done.

"The same," he said, turning back to his colleagues. "Two in front, two in back."

"The road?" Tolkien asked.

"Empty."

"Leto?" asked Fiore.

"Still inside."

"Are you sure he hasn't left?"

"Positive. His jeep is still there."

Fleming again raised the glasses and repeated his sweep, first settling on the church—a strange structure; sitting at the apex of a high, narrow peak. It looked to the Englishman, with its whitewashed walls and octagonal shape, like a child's toy teetering on a rocky stalagmite—and then on the starkly open rolling plain beyond the church to the north. "I can't for the life of me see any stone hut."

"It's there," said Fiore. "They will reach it soon."

"Could it take this long?" asked Tolkien. "D'Aquila is only ten kilometers away."

"Yes," said Fiore. "They had to go around the mountain. There is no direct road."

"Are you sure they'll have enough time to get the children there?" Tolkien asked.

"Yes," said Fiore. "They know the way through the rocks, as do the children. In ten minutes they'll be at the hut and away from here."

"And this truck will hold them all?" Tolkien asked.

"Yes," the priest replied.

Fleming rested the field glasses on his lap. He had scanned the jagged horizon compulsively for the past hour, though Fiore had told him the hut could not be seen, that it blended in, looking like any other random rock pile. It was something to do, something to take his mind off the child he had seen shot in the head that morning. "The *signal* we will see instantly," Fiore had assured him. They all eyed the exposed scree they would have to descend when they saw the signal. If the grenades didn't work, they would be quickly spotted by the guards and picked off like rabbits—large, slow rabbits.

"We'll likely be caught," said Fleming. "We should say our goodbyes."

"I'm turning myself in," said Tolkien.

"What?" Fiore and Fleming, looking sharply at the professor, said this simultaneously.

"I'll take full responsibility," said Tolkien.

"They won't believe you."

"They will."

"You'll be hung."

Tolkien said nothing. They had discussed the issue of retaliation. The Germans were known to slaughter entire towns as retribution for the slaying of just one of their officers. They had nevertheless agreed that another child killed was not to be borne, hence their plan.

"There it is," said Fiore. In the distance, from the midst of the sea of rocks and naked plain that stretched out before them, they saw a flash of light. Then two more, with five second intervals in between.

"Let's go," said Tolkien.

Each man grabbed a grenade, pulled its pin, counted to three, rose and flung it toward the rocky hill behind the church. When the grenades exploded, they grabbed their machine guns, bolted over the outcrop and began sprinting, Fleming to the rear of the church, Fiore and Tolkien toward the front.

10.
Calascio, August 4, 1943, 2 p.m.

"My men searched the cave," said Karl Wolff. "Empty. They found another nearby, also empty. Your friends must have known you would turn on them."

"They can't be far," Claudia Roselli replied.

"This map you speak of, did you see it?" Wolff asked.

"No."

"And the ring? Is it still in the Vatican?"

Claudia nodded grimly. She was beginning to doubt the wisdom of her decision. Luca in a dead sleep; alone in an unguarded cave; when else would she have such a chance? She had to take it. Now she must deal with the consequences, among them handling the arrogant, over-confident General Wolff.

She had been put into a wine cellar in Wolff's villa, its heavy oak door padlocked, and released a few moments ago for her interview with the general.

"Yes," Claudia answered.

"Then how can you help me?" said Wolff.

"I will bring you the map."

"What is your price?"

"English pounds, fifty thousand."

"How will I get that sum in this godforsaken place?"

"Send a man to Rome."

"And the key? What are your friends planning to do?"

"Small explosives, pickaxes. Improvise."

"Is Falco also searching?" Wolff asked.

"I assume he is," Claudia replied. "He must know by now that the documents I stole are missing."

"Did you read them before you gave them to me?"

"Yes, I know how important they are. I assume they are in a safe place." She was hoping that the documents Alfonso Vitale stole for her were still with Wolff. On his desk she could see a metal tube and a leather folder, both with embossed swastikas. Next to them was a silver lighter, also bearing the iconic symbol of the Nazi party, and a gold cigarette case that she knew held Wolff's French cigarettes, his favorite Gauloises.

"They are safe," Wolff replied.

Claudia nodded.

"Are you sure," said the general, "that only you and the brothers know about the map?"

"Yes."

"You've told no one else but me?"

"Yes . . . I mean no, I have told no one."

"And no one helped you find the cave you slept in last night?"

"No, the brothers seemed to know the mountains."

"The sons of Pietro Segreto, the Jew banker."

"Yes."

"Tell me about them."

"Of course, but . . ."

"But what?"

"I am filthy and hungry. I will need a change of clothes, and some food." Claudia had lost her footing several times on the hike down the mountain, scraping both knees and spraining a wrist, and then lay in a ditch for several hours until she saw the chance to approach the German camp. She was exhausted as well as dirty and hungry.

"I have rung the maid," said Wolff, who was sitting at his desk, facing the room's door. "There she is." There had been a quiet knock and now another. "Come in," Wolff said. The door swung in and Maria entered, carrying a tray of food. She nodded to Wolff, her eyes cast toward the floor. "Leave it," he said. Maria placed the tray on the desk, and stepped back.

"Maria?" said Wolff.

"Yes, Sir."

"Your aunt and uncle?"

"They are in D'Aquila still, hoping to bring my uncle to Rome. The doctor says he cannot be helped here."

"Can you handle the house by yourself?"

"Yes, but the doctor wants to be paid. Can I go to D'Aquila? I will be back by this evening."

"Who will make dinner?"

"I will have food brought up from the village."

"Yes, you can go," said the German general. "Send food for the guards as well."

Maria nodded. "Thank you, Sir."

"Go."

Claudia sat silent during this exchange, eyeing the food, but also eyeing Maria. *A beauty*, she thought. *Too skinny to be a successful whore, but a beauty nevertheless. Is she really a servant? Will she look at me?* The women glanced at each other for a second, then Maria bowed and softly left the room. She wants to kill me, Claudia said to herself. How strange.

"Now," said Wolff. "The Segreto bothers."

"Santino," Claudia replied, "the older one, is a communist. He wants to sell the bones to finance the cause." Claudia knew that this information would pique Wolff's interest. The Germans hated communism, and who could blame them? The communists in the Italian resistance, as elsewhere in Europe, had been responsible for the violent death of countless Nazi soldiers and sympathizers.

"And the younger one?" Wolff asked, drumming his fingers on his desktop.

"He wants to keep the oath, to bring the bones to a new hiding place."

"An idealist."

"A fool."

"How is it they know these mountains if they have been pampered children in Rome their whole life."

"They skied here as boys, stayed at the Gran Sasso."

"There is no skiing on the cliffs where your cave is located. Impossible terrain."

"They must have explored. The hotel is not far from here."

"Why should I trust you?"

"The night I saw you at Via Tasso, someone tried to kill me. I think it was Falco. One of his men had been following me."

"Tried to kill you how?"

"A man lunged at me with a knife. On Via Statilia. I twisted away and he fell into an old sewage ditch. I ran home."

"How do you know it was Falco?"

"He was the only one I told about the bones. I recognized the priest who was following me, his assistant, Carlo Fiore."

"Again I ask, Why should I trust you? You were playing Falco and me against each other, looking for the highest bidder."

"The Church locked me in an orphanage. Falco paid me for sex, and then to tell him my clients' secrets. Then he tried to kill me. I have had enough of the Church. I hate it. I want you to find the bones and destroy it."

"But you want money too."

"I will have to live."

"You can sell your body."

"I never sold my body."

"What did you sell, then?"

"A dream."

Claudia, her face a placid mask, was happy to see Wolff, to whom she had sold a score of dreams, smile. Her plan might work.

"How will you explain your absence?" the general asked.

"I left the cave to pee. I got lost in the dark. I slept in a ditch."

Claudia watched warily as another smile appeared on Wolff's bland, Nordic face. "Then you'd better not wash and change clothes," he said. "You can eat though. Go ahead."

On the plate were a rough-cut chunk of provolone cheese, a half loaf of thickly crusted bread, and a pile of olives. Claudia, starving, eyed the food, but controlled herself. "I'll bring it with me," she said. This was a man she had spread her legs for, but who she could not bring herself to eat in front of. Such, she realized, were the quirks of human dignity and pride, or the remnants of them. "I will take a cigarette, though."

"Of course," said the general, who extracted a Gauloise from its case, handed it to Claudia and, reaching across the desk as she leaned forward, used his silver lighter to light it for her.

"Tell me," Wolff said, after Claudia had taken a long drag and exhaled it. "If I take you up on your offer, how will you reunite with the brothers?"

"I'll go into town. Someone will get word to them."

"Why would they do that for a stranger?"

"I got lost. I slept in a ditch. The two men I am traveling with have it in their power to stop the killing of the village's children."

"I see," said Wolff, smiling again. "That should get their attention. But tell me, how do you know about the children?"

"Santino received a message at his villa. He was told about the children. We started up here immediately."

"I want the bones," said Wolff, "and I want the names of the local communists."

"I can give you both," Claudia replied. "You can stop killing children."

"Is that why you came here?" Wolff asked. "You have become soft-hearted?"

"The villagers will turn violent. It is a mistake to kill innocents."

Wolff's light-blue Aryan eyes narrowed and turned dark for a second, then he smiled. Claudia did not know if he would give the order to halt the shooting of the village's children, but she thought it best not to press her case.

"You will have to escape again," said the general.

"I will manage. They are boys. Will I be admitted when I return? There are soldiers everywhere."

"I will tell the guards to let you in, night or day."

Claudia quietly held her breath, hoping there would be no more questions. She had known Wolff for over a year, ever since he first visited Rome in 1942. She was now very happy that in that time she had never exhibited the least interest in the outcome of the war, or in anything else for that matter, except pleasing him and, of course, being paid for her services. She was a working girl, doing her best to survive. Wolff said nothing. Relieved, Claudia gathered the food and put it into the pockets of her mud-caked skirt. Nodding to the general, she began to rise to take her leave, but stopped at the sound of three loud booms that seemed to come to them from across the small valley that separated the villa from the village and the hills above it.

Wolff listened for more booms. When they didn't come, he held his hand up, palm forward. Claudia, who had half risen, sat back down. Wolff picked up the phone on his desk, but before he could dial there was a loud knock on the room's door.

"Enter."

The door swung open, and Otto Skorzeny stepped in.

"The church," he said. "I have sent troops. I will go myself."

Claudia was not the type to share a client, or even make a referral, but she survived, as whores did all over the world, on guile and gossip as well as gold. They were a sorority, the whores of Rome, a mutual benefit and protection society, passing along tidbits about good tippers, quick ejaculators and bad actors. She had heard, in the normal course of things, that Isabella Zoppi, the madam at the house she worked in when she first returned to Rome, had been shot dead by a German colonel with a red welt of a scar on his cheek. Seeing Skorzeny, she wondered if she could work him into her plan somehow.

11.

Calascio, August 4, 1943, 6 p.m.

The shepherd's hut was empty except for a stack of straw
pallets piled in a corner. Luca had extracted one of these
and was sitting on it, his back against the rough, stone wall.
Thin beams of sunlight streaming down from creases in the
thatched roof lined his dusty face. He had been trying to
sleep, but the look of contempt in his brother's eyes, and in the
woman Maria's, when they discovered that Claudia had run
off, haunted him. Could she love him so sweetly one moment
and betray him the next? How could that be? He had not
defended her, and this haunted him as well. If you loved someone, you stood up for them. She had been honest with him
about her desire to find the bones and sell them, but they were
going to do it *together*, or so she said. He knew he could talk
her out of this idea when the time came. Could she have had
some other reason for running off, or was he a special kind of
fool to love a woman who had slept with a thousand men, as
his brother had pointed out relentlessly in the last few days?

"There she is," said Santino Segreto. "One flash."

Luca rose and joined Santino at an unglazed, crudely cut
window. Within seconds two more flashes appeared in the distance. Capretta, sitting on the hut's thatched roof, called down,
"*E lei.*" After Maria had left to return to the villa, Capretta had
led them to the hut, where they were to wait for Maria to join

them, sometime in the early afternoon. At two o'clock they heard three explosions from the vicinity of Santa Maria, and could see smoke rising in the distance, first from the explosions and then from the clouds of dust kicked up by cars and trucks racing up the dirt road toward the church. With each passing hour since, their fears—that Maria was dead or injured or captured—increased. They had no food, except the bread and water that Capretta had brought, no weapons, and no means of transportation except their legs. Capretta had refused to do or say anything except sit and wait for Maria. "*Lei verra,*" was all he would say. *She will come.*

Five minutes later, she ducked under the undersized door opening and lowered the canvas sack she was carrying to the dirt floor. Wisps of her yellow hair were matted against her sweat-glazed forehead. She was dirty from the hike up the mountain, but her blue eyes were crystal clear.

"You're late," said Santino.

"What happened?" said Luca.

"Capretta," said Maria to the boy, who had leapt down and followed her into the hut, "go back to the roof. Keep a lookout." He saluted and left. In a moment his soft footsteps could be heard above.

"You are searching for the bones of Christ?" said Maria, looking from one brother to the other. "*The bones of Christ? What kind of fools are you?*"

"We are both fools, yes," Luca replied.

"Speak for yourself," said Santino.

"Your fiancée has betrayed you," said Maria.

The brothers stared at her.

"How?" said Luca.

"She was at the villa," Maria replied. "She said you had a map showing where the bones of Christ were hidden. She offered to bring it to Wolff. She offered to give him the names of the local partisans as well. She asked for fifty thousand

English pounds. She wants Wolff to use the bones to destroy the Church. She is a greedy one, your whore. She wants to get rich and destroy her most hated enemy at the same time."

"You talked to her?" said Luca.

"I overheard her talking to Wolff," said Maria. "I served her lunch."

"How did she get there?" Luca asked.

"She walked into the encampment," Maria replied. "They brought her to Wolff. They are friends, you might say. In other words, whore and client. Wolff agreed to send her back, to get the map from you."

"Let me have the map," Santino said to Luca. "I know you have it taped around your waist."

"No," Luca replied.

"What were you thinking?" Santino asked. "Were you planning on you and Claudia going off on your own to collect the bones? She always meant to rob you. You are a fool. There are Germans everywhere, and your whore—excuse me, your *fiancée*—has revealed herself for what she is."

The contempt in Santino's voice was like a blow to Luca. He knew that his newly found brother had his own plans, his own agenda, but not that he despised him. His voice was like a lash.

"Do you believe these bones really exist?" said Maria.

Neither brother answered.

"It is madness," said Maria.

"Your communism is madness," said Luca.

"Is it madness for starving people to want to eat?"

"If you won't give us the map, then you are on your own," said Santino. "Your whore will probably kill you to get it if she has to."

"I thought . . ." said Luca.

"You thought what?"

"That you wanted the bones to sell."

"I've changed my mind. I am going to kill Wolff and Leto. I will not fight you for these stupid bones."

"Leto is dead," said Maria.

The brothers stared at her.

"I stopped in town," she continued. "There was an attack on Santa Maria. The guards were killed, and Leto. Wolff has an Irish priest in custody. Two others, a priest and another Irishman, escaped and are hiding in the mountains. The priest was shot by one of the Germans guarding the church."

"The Englishmen!" said Santino.

"*Irish*," said Maria.

"Where are they?" Luca asked.

"The Irish priest is being held at Wolff's villa," Maria replied. "He goes before a firing squad tomorrow morning. The other two were found by shepherds and brought to a hiding place."

"How do you know all this?" Luca asked.

"I listen all day at the villa. That's why I work there. In town, when I do the shopping, I gather information or transmit messages. This afternoon, I was told about the two men hiding in the mountains, and I was told that your whore was looking for you," said Maria.

"She's in the town?" Luca asked.

"Wolff turned her loose so she could bring him the map. She went into town asking for help finding you and Santino."

"Where is she?" Luca asked.

"A comrade is holding her."

"Just kill her," said Santino.

"No!" said Luca.

"I think not," said Maria.

The brothers, who had been glaring at each other, turned to look at Maria.

"She can get us into the villa," said Maria. "We can kill Wolff."

Santino's glare turned into a broad smile. "Excellent," he said. "We'll kill her after we kill Wolff."

"Then I will kill *you*," said Luca.

"Fuck off, little brother."

The three of them were standing in a triangle in the tiny hut with no more than a few feet between them. Luca, his eyes hooded and dark, crouched and traversed this space so quickly that Santino had no time to react in any way. He was on his back a second later, his chest heaving, his head bleeding onto the dirt floor.

"If she dies, you die," said Luca, standing over his brother.

He stood there for another second or two, then turned and ducked out the front door. A moment later, Maria joined him.

"You love her," Maria said.

Luca did not answer immediately. He was looking at the mountains in the distance. "I am a fool," he said, finally.

"When we love we are all fools," Maria replied.

"Send for her."

"I will send Capretta, but she is going to have to help us kill Wolff. Do you agree?"

"Yes."

"She may die. You may die. We may all die."

Luca nodded. "What about the Englishman and the priest in hiding?" he said. "They could help us."

"I will have them brought here as well," said Maria. "They will want to know that their comrade is about to be executed."

12.
Calascio, August 4, 1943, 6 p.m.

"How do you find your accommodations?" said Karl Wolff.

"Splendid," John Tolkien replied.

"Feel free to uncork a bottle or two."

"I have no corkscrew."

The two men were sitting in matching chairs facing each other in the study of Wolff's confiscated villa. Tolkien had slipped on the steep dirt road as he ran down the mountain and smashed his face, which was now an angry, swollen red from temple to chin on its left side. His left eye was closed, the surrounding flesh bulging. He was bound by telegraph wire at hand and foot. Despite all this, he felt fine, unburdened of something; he could not quite say what.

"We know you had accomplices," said Wolff. "You will save your life if you tell me who they are."

Tolkien had seen Guido emerge from the church and lifted his machine gun to across his chest, the way Fleming had instructed, when Carlo Fiore appeared and in an instant mowed the Italian down. Leto's guards had returned fire and the priest had fallen to his knees. Tolkien would be executed, he knew. No information he gave Wolff could possibly change that outcome, no amount of bargaining. "I had no accomplices," he replied.

"Where did the children go?" Wolff asked.

"They must have scattered into the hills."

"There were three explosions," said Wolff.

"I had three grenades."

"Which you brought with you from Ireland."

"I told you, I am not Irish. That was a disguise. I am an Englishman."

"Professor John Tolkien, who teaches *Beowulf* at Oxford and writes children's stories."

"Yes."

"And an English spy, of course."

"Yes, but not the kind you think."

"What," said Wolff, "is this strange object?" He had been gently tapping the betrothal ring that one of Wolff's soldiers had removed from around Tolkien's neck.

"A betrothal ring," the professor answered.

"What is this thing on top?"

"A miniature of a treasure chest."

"A treasure chest?"

"Containing love and fidelity," said Tolkien. "The treasures of marriage. It was a gift from my wife on our wedding day."

"No secret compartment?"

"No."

"No poison? Cyanide?"

"No. I'm sure you've checked."

"We have. Shall I smash it open to make sure?"

"I would like to die with it around my neck."

"It is as if you wish to die," said Wolff. "You seem to look forward to it."

"I am ready to die."

"I will not bother torturing you," said Wolff. "Tomorrow morning at dawn you will be brought before a firing squad. Spies are summarily executed, and have been throughout history. Perhaps you will sleep well, perhaps not. Perhaps you will change your mind and tell me who helped you. If you do, I will send you to a prison in Rome. You will eat, sleep and live."

"I won't change my mind."

"So be it," said Wolff. "Here," he said, handing Tolkien the ring. "If there's cyanide in it, you will be saving the Reich twelve bullets."

"Thank you." Professor Tolkien took the ring on its chain from Wolff's extended hand and slipped it around his neck.

13.
Calascio, August 4, 1943, 6 p.m.

"Where is the professor?" said Carlo Fiore.

Ian Fleming shook his head. "Don't talk," he said. "Save your strength."

They were hiding behind two large boulders among many strewn about a field of tall, burnt grass—a wild Apennine landscape that was created when a glacier receded a million or so years ago. Fiore's head rested on an empty canteen. Wrapped around his abdomen was Fleming's cotton undershirt, white when it was applied, but now blood-soaked.

"You have to leave," said the priest.

"No."

"Then find my breviary."

"Your what?"

"My prayer book. It's in my pack."

Fleming did as he was told, returning to kneel once again at Fiore's side.

"Extreme unction," said Fiore, his voice a hoarse whisper. "The purple ribbon."

Fleming found the page.

"Read it," said Fiore.

"It's in Latin."

"Read it."

"In nomine Patris, et Fílii, et Spíritus Sancti, extinguatur in te omnis virtus diaboli per impositionem manuum nostrarum . . ."

Fleming looked down and saw that Fiore was slowly making the sign of the cross over his eyes, moving from them to his ears, then his nose, then his lips. He turned back to the priest's worn breviary. "*Et per invocationem gloriosae et sanctae Dei Genitricis Vírginis Marae, ejusque inclyti Sponsi Joseph, et omnium sanctorum Angelorum, Archangelorum, Martyrum, Confessorum, Vírginum, atque omnium . . .*" He looked down again and saw that the priest had rested his hands on his chest. His eyes were closed. "Carlo," he said.

"I'm resting," the priest said. "Go on."

Fleming had had enough Latin at Eton to get the gist of the prayer. He finished reading, making the sign of the cross himself over Fiore's hands and feet. "They'll be here soon," he said, when he was done. "We'll get back to Rome. I'm going to take a look." The Englishman crouched and lifted his head just above the top of the boulder that concealed them. Two old men, shepherds in bandannas and wide-brimmed hats, were stepping between two large boulders at the rim of the meadow. A young girl had come upon them as Fleming was carrying Fiore across a shallow canyon, staggering under the weight. She took them to the meadow and told them she would get help. That was two hours ago.

"It's them," Fleming said.

The priest did not respond. His eyes were closed. Fleming looked down and took Fiore's hand, which was covered with blood. "Carlo?"

"Yes," the priest replied, his raspy voice now barely audible. "I am . . ."

"What?"

"Resting."

"Help is coming."

"I have a favor . . ."

"To ask of me? Anything."

"We know the professor has the key."

Fleming nodded. "The key, yes."

"Only *he* must open the ossuary, *alone*."

"Carlo . . ."

"It is the wish of the Holy Father. You must promise me."

"I don't . . ."

"I'm dying."

Fleming could hear the footsteps of the two shepherds.

"So be it," said the Englishman. "I promise." He meant it, but he doubted the bones existed. They had just killed the head of Fascist Italy's secret police and eight elite SS troopers. He would have thus considered this mad excursion to the Apennines a complete success—were it not for the disappearance of Professor Tolkien and the wound, which he feared mortal, to Carlo Fiore's gut.

"He will survive," said Fiore.

"Who?"

"The professor."

"Of course he will. And so will you."

Carlo did not respond. He had stopped breathing.

14.
Calascio, August 4, 1943, 9 p.m.

"The servant," said Claudia Roselli, a wry smile on her face, a face that looked more, not less, angelic by virtue of the dirt that streaked it.

"How was your lunch?" Maria replied.

"Good, thank you," Claudia replied. Though she was filthy and exhausted and bound at hand and foot, she was looking at Maria with disdain, as if Maria was supposed to be the traitor, not her.

"If I had known it was for you," said Maria, "I would have poisoned it."

"Of course," said Claudia. "You have sold your soul, while I still have mine. I have sold only my body."

The two women were sitting facing each other on flat rocks in the front yard of the shepherd's hut. Santino, Luca, and Ian Fleming were on the hillside behind the hut, scraping and hacking at the mountain's rocky surface, digging a grave for Carlo Fiore's body. Capretta was on the roof. The last of the twilight was bathing the hut and its stark surroundings in a dim pink-gray. The villagers who had brought Claudia to the hut, a girl of twelve and an old man with a pistol in his hemp belt, were wending their way back down the mountain.

"We will deal with you when the priest is buried," said Maria.

"What priest?"

"Father Fiore, from the Vatican."

"Carlo Fiore?"

"I don't know his first name. Do you know him?"

"What happened?"

"They attacked the church and freed the children. He was shot in the stomach."

"Who did?"

"Two Englishmen and the priest."

"Where are the children?"

"They're safe."

"They were why I went to Wolff."

"The children?"

"I offered to bring him Luca's map. His search would be over; no need to kill children to get the townspeople to cooperate."

"Did Luca know?"

"No, he would never have agreed."

"And this I am supposed to believe?"

"Believe what you want."

"I believe you are a *putana*, and a lying one at that."

"A *putana* who can get into Wolff's villa."

"You will," said Maria, "but not because you are a saint. Because there will be a gun to your head."

"You have no choice but to do as I say," said Claudia. "They will let only me in. Once in, I will kill Wolff, then I will let you in and you can do as you like: kill the colonel living there, steal all of Wolff's papers . . ."

"You are lucky," said Maria. "One of the Englishmen is being held in the villa. He is to be shot at dawn. We will need you for more than killing Wolff."

15.
Calascio, August 4, 1943, 9:15 p.m.

Ian Fleming sat on the hard ground behind the hut, his hands clasped around his knees, his eyes closed. He longed for one of his Morlands Specials, but at night, any light, even a match or a burning cigarette, could be seen for miles in these treeless mountains. Santino and Luca Segreto sat facing him on the other side of Carlo Fiore's shallow grave. Ian and the shepherds who had helped them hide in the high meadow had taken turns carrying Carlo's body for two long, hard hours. His back ached, and so did his heart. The first thing Maria told him when he arrived at the hut was that John Tolkien was a prisoner at Wolff's villa and was to be executed at dawn. First Fiore, now Tolkien.

"I hear voices," said Luca. "I think Claudia has arrived." Female voices could indeed be heard drifting on the breeze from the front of the hut.

Santino looked at Luca, but did not respond. Luca stared back. Though night had fallen, there was more than enough starlight in the barren mountain plain for Fleming to clearly see the hatred in the brothers' eyes.

"We can't mark the grave," the Englishman said.

"No," said Santino. "We should cover it with heavy rocks. The vultures will get at it otherwise."

Fleming nodded, and was about to lift himself off the ground when Capretta appeared out of the darkness.

"Sirs," the boy said.

"You move like a ghost," said Fleming.

"Yes?" said Luca.

"The signorinas would like to talk to you," said Capretta.

"*Signorinas?*" said Luca. "Has Signorina Claudia arrived?"

"Yes."

"I will go down," said Luca.

"She wants to kill the German general," said Capretta.

All three men stared at the boy.

"And rescue your countryman," Capretta said, looking at Ian Fleming.

"*Mio connazionale?*" said Fleming. Had he heard the boy right?

"*Si,*" said Capretta. "*Il tuo connazionale.*"

16.
Calascio, August 5, 1943, 2 a.m.

"Luca," said Claudia Roselli, "are you awake?"

"Yes." They were lying on one of the straw mats, which they had brought to the rear of the hut, near Carlo Fiore's grave.

"I am pregnant."

Luca, on his back, did not answer. Claudia, still tied with rough hemp rope at hand and foot, her shoes taken from her, was lying on her side, her back to Luca.

"I know what you're thinking," said Claudia.

Luca had been looking up at the stars and continued to do so.

"You're thinking, *Whose child is it?*" said Claudia.

"Whose child *is* it?" Luca asked.

"Yours."

Luca counted the days from the first time he had made love to Claudia. A friend, another banker's son, had referred him. Going in, he was a spoiled young dilettante; coming out, he was a spoiled young dilettante in love. One night. The first before-and-after of his short life. He missed the old Luca, the one not in pain, the one who did not know that people suffered. Forty-nine days. Seven weeks. "I know there were others," he said.

"Yes," Claudia answered, "but this is your child."

"No doubt it is," said Luca. Sarcasm, he had learned, came quite easily to the lover who had been ill used.

"Why would I tell you this, Luca?" Claudia asked.

"I don't know."

"You have no money. I still want us to marry."

"You want the bones."

"Do you really want to carry them off, to hide them again, to keep your father's oath?"

"Yes."

"We're all going to die tonight."

"So be it."

"Will you marry me tonight? Now?"

"Claudia . . ."

"Signor Fleming is a naval officer. He can marry us."

"You just want me to untie you, so you can escape."

"Without shoes? My feet would be bloody stumps in a few minutes."

"You want the child to have a name."

"Yes, I do."

What was it about hearing Claudia's voice, Luca asked himself, that was as good as making love to her? Dear God.

"Go get him," said Claudia. "It will only take a minute."

Luca, looking up at the stars, felt warm tears streaming down his face.

"I want my child to have *your* name," said Claudia.

17.
Calascio, August 5, 1943, 2:15 a.m.

"How did she know you were an officer?" Maria asked.

"I've known her for some time," said Ian Fleming.

"What is your rank?"

"Commander, Royal Navy Volunteer Reserve."

"Do you know anything about ships?"

"No."

"How can that be?"

"War," Fleming replied.

"Can commanders perform marriages?"

"I'm not sure."

Fleming picked Maria's eyes out of the dark interior of the hut and wondered what she was thinking. What did it matter if these two souls were technically married or not?

"How do you know Claudia?" Maria asked.

"She worked for me in Greece."

"Is she a spy as well?"

"In a manner of speaking. She passed on information gleaned from her clients."

"She is beautiful. A well-paid whore."

"She was." Ian Fleming did not mind having a tête-à-tête with a lovely, blond Italian woman in the middle of the night in a dark, stone hut in the middle of the Apennines. When she first shook him awake, he thought she was lonely and wanted to make love, needed human contact, which put him off. He liked his women brazen or craven; anything in between was too much work.

"She loves Luca. I can see it in her eyes," said Maria.

Ah, Fleming said to himself.

"Santino and I were lovers," Maria continued.

"He's a lucky man."

"Marriage never came up."

"Some men are not the marrying type."

"I could have lured him with a child, but I didn't."

What a strange thing to say, Fleming thought. *A shotgun marriage in the middle of a guerilla war. She wants to talk.* "How did you know him?" he asked.

"I was with a communist cell fighting the fascists along the Adriatic coast, near Bari. We were trying to disrupt shipping, sabotage cargo, with not much success. Santino was a sailor going back and forth to Greece. I met him in a port bar one night. He hated Mussolini—and liked my body—and was happy to help us. He knew the shipping schedules, what cargo was vulnerable."

"And here?" Fleming asked.

"I am from D'Aquila," Maria replied. "When the Germans set up in northern Italy, the Party ordered us to come here to fight them. My aunt and uncle were servants at the villa of a wealthy family who left the country, leaving them to maintain the villa. I moved in with them. When Wolff appeared, I stayed. He thought I'd been there for years."

"*Ordered* you?"

"Yes. I am a communist. I obey orders."

"And Santino?"

"I left abruptly. He was at sea. I got word to him and he joined us a year later."

"What about the OVRA assassinations?"

"We stumbled upon an OVRA informant in D'Aquila. Before we killed him, we got the names of other informants, and the identities of OVRA agents in the region. We killed all the informants and many of the agents. Santino and a few others lived in the mountains here and around D'Aquila, mostly in caves."

Fleming said nothing. *She must still love this Santino fellow. What a burden this love business must be.*

"Santino left a week ago," Maria went on. "We were desperate for money. He said he could get some from his father. He contacted me from Rome about returning. I told him not to come back. The Germans had arrived in force and were looking for something under the castle, killing children to coerce the locals into cooperating. But he did. He came with his brother and your whore."

"And you helped them?"

"Of course."

"Why did he come back?"

"To get the bones of Christ; to sell them."

"Do they exist?"

"Something was buried under the castle hundreds of years ago. Something supernatural. This is what the local people believe. Legends start with facts, or perhaps a single fact."

"What did Santino plan on doing?"

"His father was dead; his brother had a map. He asked me to seduce his brother, to get it from him."

"Did you?"

"That was this morning."

"What if Luca tried to stop him? What would he have done?"

"I don't know. It is one thing to kill a fascist, another to kill your own brother."

"Do you know the location of the bones?"

"No. Luca still has the map."

"He's going to have to give it to Claudia if our plan is to work."

Maria nodded.

"Do you trust her?" the Englishman asked.

"We have no choice," Maria replied. For the first time, Maria looked directly at Fleming. She *was* beautiful, a blue-eyed blond in the heart of dusky Italy. Perhaps he could make an exception for such an exotic creature, torn as she was between her love for communism and her love for Santino Segreto.

"How do *you* come to be here, Commander Fleming?" Maria asked.

"The Church wants the bones, as do we," Fleming replied. "Claudia let us know. She said they were in the Church of Santa Maria della Pieta, in Calascio. Some kind of a trapdoor, a secret passage."

"She must have seen the map."

"I daresay. We drove through the night, left the car in D'Aquila and hiked into the mountains."

"You did a tremendously brave thing."

"Yes, well . . ."

"You saved thirty children."

Fleming said nothing. If there was a graph that charted the acts of bravery committed since September, 1939, to rid the world of Hitler and his madmen, his would not be on it. He threw a hand grenade and fired a machine gun. John Tolkien, on the other hand, walked into hell to divert the Germans so that he and Carlo Fiore, gravely injured, could escape. "We've lost my colleague," he said, finally.

"We will save him."

Fleming smiled ruefully. The plan was logical, but the odds of survival zero; or less, if that were possible. There were two hundred SS troops camped a kilometer away from Wolff's villa. *Change the subject, old man.* "You can still seduce Luca," he said. "He's just on the hill behind the hut. Of course, his bride is with him, but she's tied up, literally. And they may not actually be married. I don't actually know the ceremony. I mumbled through it. Richer, poorer, and so on. Everyone knows that stuff."

"Is that supposed to be British humor?"

"You can seduce me instead."

"I may. A person wants to live in the hours before they die."

"I daresay there are worse ways to spend the time."

"There is a strange look in Luca's eyes."

"Puppy love."

"He loves dogs?"

"What . . .?"

Maria laughed quietly. "No, Commander Fleming," she said. "I know what you mean. *Infatuazione giovanile.* If it were puppy love, I might try. But it's not. He is a man, a child no longer, and I will leave him to his destiny."

"As I say . . ." said Fleming.

"Yes?"

"You will find me a splendid substitute."

18.
Calascio, August 5, 1943, 3 a.m.

In two quick steps up a crooked but rock-solid ladder, Santino Segreto was on the thatched roof staring at Capretta, who had turned to look at him.

"Signor Santino," said Capretta.

"I will join you," said Santino. "I couldn't sleep. The ground was too hard."

The boy nodded, then turned to face once again the wide, gently sloping mountain plain that extended from the front of the hut as far as the eye could see, which was not far in the pitch-black, moonless night. What light there was came from the thousands of stars that littered the immense night sky.

"Your aunt Maria is angry," Santino said, when he was seated, cross-legged, next to Capretta.

"No, Signor, *sad*."

"Sad?" Santino had never heard of Maria being sad. She was a hard woman, shaped by the barren Apennines and the cruelty of the fascists who ruled Italy and persecuted her people. "She hates Claudia," he said. "She hates our plan. She's not sad."

The boy did not answer.

"You can sleep," said Santino. "I will keep watch."

A .22-caliber Berretta hunting rifle lay across Capretta's lap. Firing it would be the best way to warn the others if he saw someone approaching the hut. "You can leave the rifle," said Santino.

Capretta remained silent, making no gesture to leave the roof.

"What is it, boy?" said Santino.

"She was having your baby, Signor."

"Having my baby?"

"She killed it."

"What are you saying?"

"When you left, she went to a *jettatore* in L'Aquila. She put the evil on the baby and killed it."

"I don't believe in *il malocchio*, in *jettatore*," said Santino. "It is all superstitious nonsense."

"She has me," said Capretta. He was looking straight ahead, his voice soft.

"Of course," said Santino.

Behind them they could hear Luca and Claudia murmuring in the darkness. Below them, Fleming and Maria were sleeping on straw pallets in the hut.

"How old are you, Capretta?" Santino asked.

"I am nine."

"I am sorry about your parents."

"My parents?"

"Yes, they were killed by the Germans."

"No, Signor, my mother is alive. My father was lost at sea while I was in my mother's womb."

"Maria."

"Yes, Signor. And I believe that my father is alive and that I will meet him one day."

"What was his name?"

"Santino," said Capretta. "Like yours."

19.
Calascio, August 5, 1943, 5 a.m.

Luca Segreto and Maria were lying on their stomachs on a cliff looking down at the rear courtyard of Karl Wolff's villa some twenty meters below. Each had a machine gun resting across their arms. The flagstone-paved courtyard was itself carved out of the mountain, three of its walls sheer mountain stone, the fourth the rear wall of the villa. It was small, perhaps fifteen meters by fifteen meters. Off to their left was Ian Fleming, also armed, but also with a twenty-meter length of rope, which they hoped he had been able to secure to something on the cliff top so as to rappel down to the courtyard when the time came.

On one of the natural walls a crude swastika had been painted in white. The false dawn had come and gone and it was night again, but soon, very soon, a new day would start. A group of German soldiers were standing in front of the swastika, smoking and drinking steaming coffee from tin mugs.

"I count six," said Luca.

"Six, yes," said Maria. "Two more will lead him out, and an officer will appear, the colonel with the scarred face." A narrow, wooden door was set into the rear stone wall of the villa. "That door," Maria said, nodding. As she said this a man emerged through this door.

"There he is," said Luca.

"Scarface," said Maria.

They watched as Otto Skorzeny joined the group of soldiers and said something. One of them handed him a cigarette and lit it for him. His smoke mingled with that of the others' and drifted slowly above the courtyard before disappearing into the night.

"Have you seen this before?" Luca asked.

"Once," said Maria. "They will stand him in front of the swastika. When they do, we fire."

They extended the muzzles of their guns out over the cliff edge and waited.

20.
Calascio, August 5, 1943, 5:30 a.m.

"You have no intention of giving me any money, do you?" said Claudia Roselli, who was sitting on a wooden chair across from Karl Wolff at his desk.

"I'm afraid not," said Wolff.

"Can I leave?" Claudia asked.

"No. Not until I have had my men follow your map."

In the middle of Wolff's desk was the map, drawn in spidery ink on yellowing, curling paper, that Luca Segreto had found in old Silvano's pocket on the day he was killed by the Germans. Off to the side were the same metal cylinder and leather folder that were there yesterday, along with Wolff's silver lighter.

"It's real," said Claudia.

"We will see," said Wolff.

Claudia shrugged. "Of course."

"In the meantime . . ." said Wolff, smiling and reaching for his belt buckle.

"So early?" said Claudia.

"You know I am *verhornt* early in the morning," said Wolff. "It is your fault for knocking at my door at 5 a.m." The general now had his belt unbuckled and the fly of his uniform pants unzipped. He gently rubbed his crotch and then began to reach inside his underpants.

"Can I freshen?" Claudia asked.

"*Sicher*," said the general, smiling and nodding to a door to the right. "I like you freshened."

"*Danke*, Herr General," said Claudia, effecting a demure curtsy.

Once inside the bathroom Claudia turned on a faucet and reached for the small pistol she had tucked into the waistband of her skirt. She was supposed to wait until she heard firing in the courtyard, but she would have to go ahead and hope for the best. She undid the buttons on her blouse, then took off her skirt and draped it over the gun. As she reached for the doorknob there was a knocking on the door and it swung open. Karl Wolff stood there, a broad smile on his face, his pants and underwear at his ankles. Claudia faked a smile and was about to say something when she heard the sharp staccato of machine-gun fire. She extended her right arm, as if she was handing Wolff her skirt, and shot the general three times in the chest.

Stepping over Wolff, Claudia buttoned her blouse, scrambled into her skirt, and moved quickly to his desk, where she first grabbed Luca's map and shoved it into her bra. She then opened the metal cylinder, looked inside and tossed it aside. A quick glance into the leather folder revealed the documents poor Alfonso Vitale had stolen for her on the basis of a whore's empty promises, a whore who no longer existed. She picked up Wolff's lighter and set these documents on fire. She made sure they were fully aflame, then headed for the villa's front door, where she hoped to be greeted by Santino Segreto and not the barrels of German machine guns.

21.
Calascio, August 5, 1943, 5:30 a.m.

Maria and Luca surveyed the scene below: seven Germans sprawled on the flagstone courtyard, Professor John Tolkien curled on his side under the swastika, Ian Fleming leaping from the end of a rope. They had had to wait for Tolkien to be placed against the swastika wall before firing. Until then he and the soldiers were in too close proximity to risk it. They might have killed him as well.

"One is moving," said Luca, aiming his machine gun.

"No!" said Maria, "don't shoot. The professor is right behind him."

As Luca drew his gun back, the German who had been moving lay still again. He was directly in front of Tolkien. They watched as Fleming sprinted to his colleague, turned him onto his back, then lifted him into his arms. "He's alive," Fleming shouted. "I'm taking him through the house. Get going."

Maria and Luca rose and were about to run, when the German who had first moved suddenly got to his feet with a rifle in his hands, aimed at them. Fleming and Tolkien were directly behind him. Luca aimed at the German but then, afraid of hitting the Englishmen, moved to the side to aim again. As he did this, the German fired and Luca spilled head-first onto the courtyard's flagstone floor. Before the German could fire again, Maria leapt down and crashed onto him, knocking him to the ground. Seeing this unfold, Fleming laid Tolkien down and lifted his own machine gun. The soldier leapt to his feet and began looking for his rifle, which the force of Maria's blow had catapulted from his hands.

"Scarface," said Fleming, before firing a full clip into Otto Skorzeny. "Hell is too good for you." He then went over to Maria, who lay on her back, bleeding heavily from a large gash at her hairline. He quickly put his ear to her lips and two fingers to her jugular. She was dead. He smoothed the hair away from her face, closed her eyes and composed her body as best he could, then turned to Luca, who had an entry wound in the center of his forehead. Fleming brushed Luca's eyes shut as well, then turned to Tolkien, who was sitting up.

"Am I alive?" the professor said.

"You're alive."

"You're not Saint Peter?"

"No. What happened?"

"I was thrown against the wall somehow, hit my head." The professor put his hand to the back of his head. When he took it away it was covered with blood.

"Your face as well?" Tolkien asked.

"No, I fell on the road after we attacked the church."

Fleming smiled grimly. "We're going back there," he said. "Can you climb that rope?" He pointed to the far wall. "We have to get out of here."

22.
Calascio, August 5, 1943, 5:30 a.m.

Santino Segreto saw Claudia Roselli emerge from the villa, but she was a blur. No matter what he did he could not rub his eyes clear and could not stop the ringing in his ears. He had hiked in the dark with Claudia to a point halfway up the steep road that led to the villa, then dropped down to a rocky shelf where he stood and watched her approach the guards at the gate. One of them escorted her in and returned to his post a few minutes later. When he heard the machine-gun fire at the rear of the villa, he did as planned. He leapt back up to the road and rushed the guards, running low and under control so that he could fire his machine gun in a tight arc back and forth at the two guards. One went down, but the other dropped to a knee and fired back. Santino kept running and firing, but things slowed down and the next he knew he was lying on the ground, rubbing hot liquid from his eyes. For the life of him, he could not move.

Then suddenly Claudia was kneeling over him, wiping his eyes clear, and placing something on his chest. Her hand? It felt good.

"Santino, can you get up?"

Santino shook his head, the slight side-to-side movement sending lightning bolts of pain into his brain and blurring his vision again.

"I will drag you."

"I'm dying," he said.

"No."

"Go."

"No."

"I'm sorry," he said.

"For what?"

"For hating you and Luca." Was she crying? "I remember you," he said.

"Yes, Figaro. I remember you too. I thought you had died."

"No, but I am dying now."

"You said nothing," said Claudia.

"My brother loves you. He did not need to know about us."

"Thank you."

"Did you . . .?"

"Yes. I killed Wolff. I have the map."

"Claudia?"

"Yes?"

"Capretta . . ."

"Yes?"

"He is my son."

"Your son?"

"Yes. Take care of him, please. And Luca too, if he lives."

∞∞∞∞ ∞∞∞∞ ∞∞∞∞

Claudia heard a series of explosions coming from the vicinity of the German encampment and knew that it was under attack, that Capretta had done his part—persuaded what partisans he could to harass and therefore distract the nearby soldiers and their officers. She looked down at Santino Segreto. The side of his head had been blown off. The bleeding that had clogged his eyes had slowed to a trickle. She placed her hand against his heart again. He was dead. She closed his eyes, rose, and headed for the Church of Santa Maria della Pieta, two kilometers away.

262

23.

Calascio, August 5, 1943, 6:30 a.m.

"Where are we, do you think?" said John Tolkien.

"I'd say just beneath the castle." Torch in hand, Fleming was looking down at Luca's map.

"I don't see any markings," said Tolkien. He too had a flashlight and was pointing it up to the long tunnel's rocky ceiling. "The map says to go one thousand steps. People may have taken smaller steps in 1453."

"Or longer," said Fleming.

"There's another pitch basket," said Tolkien, shining the beam of his torch on a small, latticed container hanging from a rusted, cast-iron ring embedded in the rocky ceiling. They had seen four or five of these en route, and surmised that they were meant to hold pitch to light the way in what they further surmised was an ancient escape passage from the castle to the church, or vice versa. "Let's keep going."

Crouching—the tunnel ceiling was no more than five feet overhead—they slowly moved forward, but after only twenty steps or so ran into a pile of large stones that started at the ceiling and sloped gradually down to their feet. They could go no further.

"That may have been the way up to the castle," said Tolkien.

"Bloody hell," said Fleming. "I need to sit."

"Not too long," said Tolkien. "Our German friends are sure to be insanely active right about now."

"Capretta said he warned the villagers," said Fleming. "Let's hope they're all in the mountains."

"Pray," said Tolkien.

Fleming nodded. He had slumped against the tunnel wall and Tolkien had joined him. They were both filthy and tired, but in no hurry to greet whatever awaited them in the world above.

"Speaking of prayer . . ." said Fleming.

"Yes?"

"How is it done?"

"That's a silly question," said the professor. "Better to ask why."

"Do you still believe in it?"

"Are you thinking of converting?" asked Tolkien.

"Have you converted back?"

"My goodness," said Tolkien.

"I've been worried about you."

"I would think you'd be happy."

"Gloating, you mean."

"I wouldn't go that far."

"I'll tell you straight out," said Fleming. "I cannot be a cad if you lose your faith."

Tolkien smiled broadly, the soot lines creasing his face. "There is a just God," he said, "who loves us. You pray by talking to him. You will find yourself immediately humbled. You will find that the thing you thought you were does not exist; that it never existed."

"You wanted to die," said Fleming.

Tolkien did not answer at first. "I'm over that now," he said finally.

"You saved my life."

"And mine," said Tolkien.

Fleming leaned his head against the rock wall. "I wish I had a cigarette."

"And I my—"

"Did you hear that?" Fleming interrupted.

"Yes," Tolkien replied.

Something had fallen and they had heard it hit the ground. They both shined their torches, floor to ceiling, back along the way they had come.

"More loose rock," said Fleming.

"Look," said Tolkien. He had placed the beam of his torch on the pitch basket they had just passed under. It seemed to be moving slightly. "Let's have a look."

Standing under the basket, shining their lights on it, they could see that it was filled with small stones. One perhaps had fallen out. All the pitch baskets they had seen were old and decrepit. Some still held the stones that they surmised retained the pitch that was lit when the tunnel was used. As they looked up, another stone fell directly onto John Tolkien's head. Laughing, he reached up to shake the rest of the stones out. As he grabbed the basket, a large amount of dirt that had caked over the centuries on the ceiling came loose and descended on them like a black cloud. They swept at this cloud with their hands and then rubbed dirt and cinders from their eyes. When they looked up they saw a thin beam of light breaking through the ceiling near the cast-iron ring from which the basket hung. Tolkien reached up and removed the basket. Shining their torches they could see that the ring hung from a wooden door.

24.

Calascio, August 5, 1943, 6:30 a.m.

Claudia Roselli and Capretta had climbed to the domed roof of the church of Santa Maria della Pieta, the better to survey the country around them, which was crawling with Germans on foot and in jeeps and small trucks. The day had been clear and bright at sunrise, but a steady rain had begun as they made their way to the catwalk that rimmed the dome. The weather had been so hot and dry all summer that this rain had quickly turned the dirt road leading to the church into a stream of mud. Soon it would be impassable, which was a good thing, because, though the SS search parties had thus far ignored the church, they were sure to want to get around to it before long. The village of Calascio below and to their right was empty, its two hundred inhabitants having melted before dawn into the surrounding mountains.

To their left, in the church's rear courtyard, they could see the pile of rubble that had once been the well that a hundred years ago supplied the church with water. When the Englishmen arrived, they had all scraped at this pile to expose the entrance to the tunnel that had been marked on Luca Segreto's map. Rain and mud from the hillside behind it was beginning to spill into this maw.

"I will cover it," said Capretta. "There are planks in a room behind the altar."

Claudia watched as the little goat scrambled lithely down the side of the church. She prayed that the tunnel would not flood, nor the Germans arrive, before Signori Tolkien and Fleming returned.

25.

Calascio, August 5, 1943, 6:30 a.m.

The room that Ian Fleming had hoisted John Tolkien into was pitch black. If he hadn't had his flashlight, Tolkien would have been lost in darkness, completely sightless. Where the beam of light came from that he and Fleming had both seen piercing the tunnel ceiling near the cast-iron ring he could not guess, except perhaps from the God with whom he had moments before reunited. Scanning the tiny room was a moment's work. He went around once, floor to ceiling, to confirm its total emptiness before returning to the small, stone box on a shelf cut into the far wall.

As he drew closer he saw that the box had a crude cross etched onto its front surface, above which was a small, square opening. He removed the betrothal ring from around his neck and inserted it into this opening. When he turned it to the left, he heard a click and the stone lid opened an inch or two. With the torch in his left hand, he placed the fingers of his right hand under the lid. He raised it another inch or so, then stopped. He could see a beautiful, golden-yellow light glowing inside the box. He closed the lid, removed the key and put it around his neck.

26.

Calascio, August 5, 1943, 6:45 a.m.

Capretta had covered the tunnel entrance with old planking he had found in the church's storeroom and returned to the roof, where he and Claudia stood now watching as torrents of rain and mud found their way around and through the planks into the tunnel, which in a few minutes would cease to be a tunnel and would become a drowning pool, a watery grave for two brave men. Behind them the road to the church was completely washed out, which was some consolation, but not much.

"Look," said Capretta.

Claudia turned and saw two German half-tracks staging at the bottom of the road. One lined up behind the other and then they started chugging up the road, splashing curtains of mud left and right.

"Is there a way out of here?" Claudia asked.

"Yes," the boy replied. "Beyond the hill is a canyon. It cuts through to caves on the other side. They will not find us."

Claudia looked down at the half-tracks. They were nearly halfway to the church.

"Look!" said Capretta.

Claudia turned back to see Fleming and Tolkien pushing away the planks and emerging from the tunnel. She was never happier in her life to see two filthy, mud-soaked men. Before she could speak, Capretta was on the ground, running through the pouring rain. Claudia rapidly followed, jumping the last ten feet and falling into a pool of mud, then scrambling to her feet to join the boy and the men.

"What's that noise?" said Fleming.

"Half-tracks," said Capretta. "Follow me."

He leaped over the well rubble and began scrambling up the hill that separated the churchyard from the mountains. Tolkien, Fleming and Claudia followed. When they reached the top, they felt the ground beneath them begin to tremble. In front of them was a raging stream; beyond the stream, the narrow opening to a canyon gouged out of the mountain before history began.

"Jump," said Capretta.

They leapt as one over the stream and raced for the canyon.

Behind them, though they did not see it, the hill behind the Church of Santa Maria della Pieta was disintegrating, becoming a lava-like mudslide that obliterated the well rubble, the planks and the tunnel opening. It rolled right into the half-tracks as they were turning the church's corner to enter the rear courtyard, stopping them completely, mud up to their windows.

Epilogue
Ischia, August 15, 1952, 5 p.m.

Claudia Roselli stood on the small porch at the back of her whitewashed bungalow, lightly clutching the Jewish betrothal ring she wore around her neck, running the tip of her index finger over the gemstone cross on its flat surface. Nearby, attached to a wooden post, was the bell she rang to call her children in from play. She could see them now, Santino and Luca, on the beach. Santino, who she stopped calling Capretta years ago, tall and bronzed, with flowing blond hair like his mother's, stood like an Olympian god and watched as Luca, who had turned eight in April, ran in and out of the surf.

Today was the Feast of the Assumption, celebrating the death of the Virgin Mary and her assumption into heaven. That morning, Father Gerard had stopped by to bless the sea behind her house. She did not know Santino's birthday and neither did he, so she years ago assigned him August 15, in honor of the Blessed Mother. Today he turned eighteen. Today she would tell him who he was, and who she was. She would not tell him of the oath that had killed his father and Luca's father.

She had not asked *il Professore* Tolkien if he had found the bones of Christ. She did not have to. In the days she and Capretta spent with the two Englishmen in the mountains before escaping to Rome, and then Naples, she saw it in his eyes. There was, for certain, a just and merciful God who loved us, and his son was Jesus Christ, who lived among us for a short time two thousand years ago, and whose bones—or per-haps his divine spirit—lay in a small box under a mountain in the heart of Italy.

She reached for the bell.

About the Authors

James LePore is an attorney who has practiced law for more than two decades. He is also an accomplished photographer. He lives in South Salem, NY with his wife, artist Karen Chandler. He is the author of five solo novels, *A World I Never Made*, *Blood of My Brother*, *Sons and Princes*, *Gods and Fathers*, and *The Fifth Man*, as well as a collection of three short stories, *Anyone Can Die* and the first two novels in the Mythmakers Trilogy, *No Dawn for Men* and *God's Formula*. You can visit him at his website, www.James-LeporeFiction.com.

Carlos Davis writes and produces films, among them the Emmy nominated *Rascals & Robbers* with David Taylor and the global cult favorite *Drop Dead Fred* with Tony Fingleton, which they produced with Working Title Films. His next film project is his screenplay, *Betsy and Napoleon*, about the Emperor's last years on St. Helena. He is producing that project with Marcia Nasatir and Fred Roos. He and novelist James Lepore wrote the national bestseller, *No Dawn For Men* that was a finalist for the International Thriller Award. The thriller's sequel, *God's Formula* was published last year. He lives in New York City.